D0103897

Autobiography and Interviews

Speak, Memory: An Autobiography Revisited
Strong Opinions

Biography and Criticism

Nikolai Gogol
Lectures on Literature
Lectures on Russian Literature
Lectures on Don Quixote

Translations

Three Russian Poets:
Translations of Pushkin, Lermontov, and Tyutchev
A Hero of Our Time (Mikhail Lermontov)
The Song of Igor's Campaign (Anon.)
Eugene Onegin (Alexander Pushkin)

Letters

The Nabokov–Wilson Letters: Correspondence between
Vladimir Nabokov and Edmund Wilson, 1940–1971
Vladimir Nabokov: Selected Letters, 1940–1977

Miscellaneous

Poems and Problems
The Annotated Lolita

VINTAGE NABOKOV

Vladimir Nabokov

VINTAGE BOOKS

A Division of Random House, Inc.

New York

The pieces in this collection were published as follows:

"The Return of Chorb," "The Aurelian," "Russian Spoken Here,"
"Cloud, Castle, Lake," "Mademoiselle O," "A Forgotten Poet,"
"Time and Ebb," "Signs and Symbols," "The Vane Sisters," and
"Lance" from *The Stories of Vladimir Nabokov,* copyright © 1995
by Dmitri Nabokov (Alfred A. Knopf, 1995). The selection
from *Lolita,* copyright © 1955 by Vladimir Nabokov (Olympia Press, Paris,
1955 and Putnam, New York, 1958). The selection from *Speak, Memory,*
copyright © 1951, 1967 by Vladimir Nabokov (Harper & Bros., 1951
and Putnam, 1967).

Library of Congress Cataloging-in-Publication Data
Nabokov, Vladimir Vladimirovich, 1899–1977.
[Selections. 2004]
Vintage Nabokov / Vladimir Nabokov.—1st Vintage Books ed.
p.   cm.
ISBN: 1-4000-3401-9
I. Title.
PS3527.A15A6 2004
813'.54—dc21   2003057572

Book design by JoAnne Metsch

www.vintagebooks.com

CONTENTS

THE RETURN OF CHORB
from *The Stories of Vladimir Nabokov*   3

THE AURELIAN
from *The Stories of Vladimir Nabokov*   14

RUSSIAN SPOKEN HERE
from *The Stories of Vladimir Nabokov*   30

CLOUD, CASTLE, LAKE
from *The Stories of Vladimir Nabokov*   42

MADEMOISELLE O
from *The Stories of Vladimir Nabokov*   52

Selection from *Lolita*   71

A FORGOTTEN POET
from *The Stories of Vladimir Nabokov*   108

TIME AND EBB
from *The Stories of Vladimir Nabokov*   123

SIGNS AND SYMBOLS
from *The Stories of Vladimir Nabokov*   132

THE VANE SISTERS
from *The Stories of Vladimir Nabokov*   139

LANCE
from *The Stories of Vladimir Nabokov*   157

Chapter Twelve from *Speak, Memory*   172

VINTAGE NABOKOV

THE RETURN OF CHORB

The Kellers left the opera house at a late hour. In that pacific German city, where the very air seemed a little lusterless and where a transverse row of ripples had kept shading gently the reflected cathedral for well over seven centuries, Wagner was a leisurely affair presented with relish so as to overgorge one with music. After the opera Keller took his wife to a smart nightclub renowned for its white wine. It was past one in the morning when their car, flippantly lit on the inside, sped through lifeless streets to deposit them at the iron wicket of their small but dignified private house. Keller, a thickset old German, closely resembling Oom Paul Kruger, was the first to step down on the sidewalk, across which the loopy shadows of leaves stirred in the streetlamp's gray glimmer. For an instant his starched shirtfront and the droplets of bugles trimming his wife's dress caught the light as she disengaged a stout leg and climbed out of the car in her turn. The maid met them in the vestibule and, still carried by the momentum of the news, told them in a frightened whisper about Chorb's having called. Frau Keller's chubby face, whose everlasting freshness somehow agreed with her Russian merchant-class parentage, quivered and reddened with agitation.

"He said she was ill?"

The maid whispered still faster. Keller stroked his gray brush of hair with his fat palm, and an old man's frown overcast his large, somewhat simian face, with its long upper lip and deep furrows.

"I simply refuse to wait till tomorrow," muttered Frau Keller, shaking her head as she gyrated heavily on one spot, trying to catch the end of the veil that covered her auburn wig. "We'll go there at once. Oh dear, oh dear! No wonder there's been no letters for quite a month."

Keller punched his gibus open and said in his precise, slightly guttural Russian: "The man is insane. How dare he, if she's ill, take her a second time to that vile hotel?"

But they were wrong, of course, in thinking that their daughter was ill. Chorb said so to the maid only because it was easier to utter. In point of fact he had returned alone from abroad and only now realized that, like it or not, he would have to explain how his wife had perished, and why he had written nothing about it to his in-laws. It was all very difficult. How was he to explain that he wished to possess his grief all by himself, without tainting it by any foreign substance and without sharing it with any other soul? Her death appeared to him as a most rare, almost unheard-of occurrence; nothing, it seemed to him, could be purer than such a death, caused by the impact of an electric stream, the same stream which, when poured into glass receptacles, yields the purest and brightest light.

Ever since that spring day when, on the white highway a dozen kilometers from Nice, she had touched, laughing, the live wire of a storm-felled pole, Chorb's entire world ceased to sound like a world: it retreated at once, and even the dead body that he carried in his arms to the nearest village struck him as something alien and needless.

In Nice, where she had to be buried, the disagreeable consumptive clergyman kept in vain pressing him for details: Chorb responded only with a languid smile. He sat daylong on the shingly beach, cupping colored pebbles and letting them flow from hand to hand; and then, suddenly, without waiting for the funeral, he traveled back to Germany.

He passed in reverse through all the spots they had visited together during their honeymoon journey. In Switzerland where they had wintered and where the apple trees were now in their last bloom, he recognized nothing except the hotels. As to the Black Forest, through which they had hiked in the preceding autumn, the chill of the spring did not impede memory. And just as he had tried, on the southern beach, to find again that unique rounded black pebble with the regular little white belt, which she had happened to show him on the eve of their last ramble, so now he did his best to look up all the roadside items that retained her exclamation mark: the special profile of a cliff, a hut roofed with a layer of silvery-gray scales, a black fir tree and a footbridge over a white torrent, and something which one might be inclined to regard as a kind of fatidic prefiguration: the radial span of a spider's web between two telegraph wires that were beaded with droplets of mist. She accompanied him: her little boots stepped rapidly, and her hands never stopped moving, moving—to pluck a leaf from a bush or stroke a rock wall in passing—light, laughing hands that knew no repose. He saw her small face with its dense dark freckles, and her wide eyes, whose pale greenish hue was that of the shards of glass licked smooth by the sea waves. He thought that if he managed to gather all the little things they had noticed together—if he re-created thus the near past—her image would grow immortal and replace her forever. Nighttime, though, was unendurable. Night imbued with sudden terror her irrational presence. He hardly slept at all during the three weeks of his trek—and now he got off, quite drugged with fatigue, at the railway station, which had been last autumn their point of departure from the quiet town where he had met and married her.

It was around eight o'clock of the evening. Beyond the houses the cathedral tower was sharply set off in black against a golden-red stripe of sunset. In the station square stood in file the selfsame decrepit fiacres. The identical newspaper seller uttered his hollow crepuscular cry. The same black poodle with apathetic eyes was in the act of raising a thin hindleg near a Morris pillar, straight at the scarlet lettering of a playbill announcing *Parsifal*.

Chorb's luggage consisted of a suitcase and a big tawny trunk. A fiacre took him through the town. The cabby kept indolently flapping his reins, while steadying the trunk with one hand. Chorb remembered that she whom he never named liked to take rides in cabs.

In a lane at the corner of the municipal opera house there was an old three-storied hotel of a disreputable type with rooms that were let by the week, or by the hour. Its black paint had peeled off in geographical patterns; ragged lace curtained its bleary windows; its inconspicuous front door was never locked. A pale but jaunty lackey led Chorb down a crooked corridor reeking of dampness and boiled cabbage into a room which Chorb recognized—by the picture of a pink *baigneuse* in a gilt frame over the bed—as the very one in which he and his wife had spent their first night together. Everything amused her then—the fat man in his shirtsleeves who was vomiting right in the passage, and the fact of their having chosen by chance such a beastly hotel, and the presence of a lovely blond hair in the washbasin; but what tickled her most was the way they had escaped from her house. Immediately upon coming home from church she ran up to her room to change, while downstairs the guests were gathering for supper. Her father, in a dress coat of sturdy cloth, with a flabby grin on his apish face, clapped this or that man on the shoulder and served ponies of brandy himself. Her mother, in the meantime, led her closest friends, two by two, to inspect the bedroom meant for the young couple: with tender emotion, whispering under her breath, she pointed out the colossal eiderdown, the orange blossoms, the two pairs of brand-new bedroom slippers—large checkered ones, and tiny red ones with pompons—that she had aligned on the bedside rug, across which a Gothic inscription ran: "WE ARE TOGETHER UNTO THE TOMB." Presently, everybody moved toward the hors d'oeuvres—and Chorb and his wife, after the briefest of consultations, fled through the back door, and only on the following morning, half an hour before the express train was to leave, reappeared to collect their luggage. Frau Keller had sobbed all night; her husband, who had always regarded Chorb (destitute Russian émigré and littérateur) with suspicion, now cursed his daughter's choice, the cost of the liquor, the local police that could do nothing. And several times, after the Chorbs had gone, the old man went to look at the hotel in the lane behind the opera house, and henceforward that black, purblind house became an object of disgust and attraction to him like the recollection of a crime.

While the trunk was being brought in, Chorb kept staring at the rosy chromo. When the door closed, he bent over the trunk and unlocked it. In a corner of the room, behind a loose strip of wallpaper, a mouse made a scuffing noise and then raced like a toy on rollers. Chorb turned on his heel with a start. The lightbulb hanging from the ceiling on a cord swayed ever so gently, and the shadow of the cord glided across the green couch and broke at its edge. It was on that couch that he had slept on his nuptial night. She, on the regular bed, could be heard breathing with the even rhythm of a child. That night he had kissed her once—on the hollow of the throat—that had been all in the way of lovemaking.

The mouse was busy again. There exist small sounds that are more frightening than gunfire. Chorb left the trunk alone and paced the room a couple of times. A moth struck the lamp with a ping. Chorb wrenched the door open and went out.

On the way downstairs he realized how weary he was, and when he found himself in the alley the blurry blue of the May night made him dizzy. Upon turning into the boulevard he walked faster. A square. A stone *Herzog*. The black masses of the City Park. Chestnut trees now were in flower. *Then,* it had been autumn. He had gone for a long stroll with her on the eve of the wedding. How good was the earthy, damp, somewhat violety smell of the dead leaves strewing the sidewalk! On those enchanting overcast days the sky would be of a dull white, and the small twig-reflecting puddle in the middle of the black pavement resembled an insufficiently developed photograph. The gray-stone villas were separated by the mellow and motionless foliage of yellowing trees, and in front of the Kellers' house the leaves of a withering poplar had acquired the tone of transparent grapes. One glimpsed, too, a few birches behind the bars of the gate; ivy solidly muffed some of their boles, and Chorb made a point of telling her that ivy never grew on birches in Russia, and she remarked that the foxy tints of their minute leaves reminded her of spots of tender rust upon ironed linen. Oaks and chestnuts lined the sidewalk; their black bark was velveted with green rot; every now and then a leaf broke away to fly athwart the street like a scrap of wrapping paper. She attempted to catch it on the wing by means of a child's spade found near a heap of pink bricks at a spot where the street was under repair.

A little way off the funnel of a workers' van emitted gray-blue smoke which drifted aslant and dissolved between the branches—and a resting workman, one hand on his hip, contemplated the young lady, as light as a dead leaf, dancing about with that little spade in her raised hand. She skipped, she laughed. Chorb, hunching his back a bit, walked behind her—and it seemed to him that happiness itself had that smell, the smell of dead leaves.

At present he hardly recognized the street, encumbered as it was with the nocturnal opulence of chestnut trees. A streetlamp glinted in front; over the glass a branch drooped, and several leaves at its end, saturated with light, were quite translucent. He came nearer. The shadow of the wicket, its checkerwork all distorted, swept up toward him from the sidewalk to entangle his feet. Beyond the gate, and beyond a dim gravel walk, loomed the front of the familiar house, dark except for the light in one open window. Within that amber chasm the housemaid was in the act of spreading with an ample sweep of her arms a snow-bright sheet on a bed. Loudly and curtly Chorb called out to her. With one hand he still gripped the wicket and the dewy touch of iron against his palm was the keenest of all memories.

The maid was already hurrying toward him. As she was to tell Frau Keller later, what struck her first was the fact that Chorb remained standing silently on the sidewalk although she had unlocked the little gate at once. "He had no hat," she related, "and the light of the streetlamp fell on his forehead, and his forehead was all sweaty, and the hair was glued to it by the sweat. I told him master and mistress were at the theater. I asked him why he was alone. His eyes were blazing, their look terrified me, and he seemed not to have shaved for quite a time. He said softly: 'Tell them that she is ill.' I asked: 'Where are you staying?' He said: 'Same old place,' and then added: 'That does not matter. I'll call again in the morning.' I suggested he wait—but he didn't reply and went away."

Thus Chorb traveled back to the very source of his recollections, an agonizing and yet blissful test now drawing to a close. All there remained was but a single night to be spent in that first chamber of their marriage, and by tomorrow the test would be passed and her image made perfect.

But as he trudged back to the hotel, up the boulevard, where on all the benches in the blue darkness sat hazy figures, Chorb suddenly understood that, despite exhaustion, he would not be able to sleep alone in that room with its naked bulb and whispery crannies. He reached the square and plodded along the city's main avenue—and now he knew what must be done. His quest, however, lasted a long while: This was a quiet and chaste town, and the secret by-street where one could buy love was unknown to Chorb. Only after an hour of helpless wandering, which caused his ears to sing and his feet to burn, did he enter that little lane—whereupon he accosted at once the first girl who hailed him.

"The night," said Chorb, scarcely unclenching his teeth.

The girl cocked her head, swung her handbag, and replied: "Twenty-five."

He nodded. Only much later, having glanced at her casually, Chorb noted with indifference that she was pretty enough, though considerably jaded, and that her bobbed hair was blond.

She had been in that hotel several times before, with other customers, and the wan, sharp-nosed lackey, who was tripping down as they were going upstairs, gave her an amiable wink. While Chorb and she walked along the corridor, they could hear, from behind one of the doors, a bed creaking, rhythmically and weightily, as if a log were being sawed in two. A few doors farther the same monotonous creak came from another room, and as they passed by the girl looked back at Chorb with an expression of cold playfulness.

In silence he ushered her into his room—and immediately, with a profound anticipation of sleep, started to tear off his collar from its stud. The girl came up very close to him: "And what about a small present?" she suggested, smiling.

Dreamily, absentmindedly, Chorb considered her, as he slowly grasped what she meant.

Upon receiving the banknotes, she carefully arranged them in her bag, uttered a light little sigh, and again rubbed herself against him.

"Shall I undress?" she asked with a shake of her bob.

"Yes, go to bed," muttered Chorb. "I'll give you some more in the morning."

The girl began to undo hastily the buttons of her blouse, and kept glancing at him askance, being slightly taken aback by his abstraction and gloom. He shed his clothes quickly and carelessly, got into the bed, and turned to the wall.

"This fellow likes kinky stuff," vaguely conjectured the girl. With slow hands she folded her chemise, placed it upon a chair. Chorb was already fast asleep.

The girl wandered around the room. She noticed that the lid of the trunk standing by the window was slightly ajar; by squatting on her heels, she managed to peep under the lid's edge. Blinking and cautiously stretching out her bare arm, she palpated a woman's dress, a stocking, scraps of silk—all this stuffed in anyhow and smelling so nice that it made her feel sad.

Presently she straightened up, yawned, scratched her thigh, and, just as she was, naked, but in her stockings, drew aside the window curtain. Behind the curtain the casement was open and one could make out, in the velvety depths, a corner of the opera house, the black shoulder of a stone Orpheus outlined against the blue of the night, and a row of light along the dim façade which slanted off into darkness. Down there, far away, diminutive dark silhouettes swarmed as they emerged from bright doorways onto the semicircular layers of illumined porch steps, to which glided up cars with shimmering headlights and smooth glistening tops. Only when the breakup was over and the brightness gone, the girl closed the curtain again. She switched off the light and stretched on the bed beside Chorb. Just before falling asleep she caught herself thinking that once or twice she had already been in that room: she remembered the pink picture on its wall.

Her sleep lasted not more than an hour: a ghastly deep-drawn howl roused her. It was Chorb screaming. He had woken up sometime after midnight, had turned on his side, and had seen his wife lying beside him. He screamed horribly, with visceral force. The white specter of a woman sprang off the bed. When, trembling, she turned on the light, Chorb was sitting among the tumbled bedclothes, his back to the wall, and through his spread fingers one eye could be seen burning with a mad flame. Then he slowly uncovered his face, slowly recognized the girl. With a frightened mutter she was hastily putting on her chemise.

And Chorb heaved a sigh of relief, for he realized that the ordeal was over. He moved onto the green couch, and sat there, clasping his hairy shins and with a meaningless smile contemplating the harlot. That smile increased her terror; she turned away, did up one last hook, laced her boots, busied herself with the putting on of her hat.

At this moment the sound of voices and footsteps came from the corridor.

One could hear the voice of the lackey repeating mournfully: "But look here, there's a lady with him." And an irate guttural voice kept insisting: "But I'm telling you she's my daughter."

The footsteps stopped at the door. A knock followed.

The girl snatched her bag from the table and resolutely flung the door open. In front of her stood an amazed old gentleman in a lusterless top hat, a pearl stud gleaming in his starched shirt. From over his shoulder peered the tear-stained face of a stout lady with a veil on her hair. Behind them the puny pale lackey strained up on tiptoe, making big eyes and gesturing invitingly. The girl understood his signs and shot out into the corridor, past the old man, who turned his head in her wake with the same puzzled look and then crossed the threshold with his companion. The door closed. The girl and the lackey remained in the corridor. They exchanged a frightened glance and bent their heads to listen. But in the room all was silence. It seemed incredible that inside there should be three people. Not a single sound came from there.

"They don't speak," whispered the lackey, and put his fingers to his lips.

THE AURELIAN

1

Luring aside one of the trolley-car numbers, the street started at the corner of a crowded avenue. For a long time it crept on in obscurity, with no shopwindows or any such joys. Then came a small square (four benches, a bed of pansies) round which the trolley steered with rasping disapproval. Here the street changed its name, and a new life began. Along the right side, shops appeared: a fruiterer's, with vivid pyramids of oranges; a tobacconist's, with the picture of a voluptuous Turk; a delicatessen, with fat brown and gray coils of sausages; and then, all of a sudden, a butterfly store. At night, and especially when it was damp, with the asphalt shining like the back of a seal, passersby would stop for a second before that symbol of fair weather. The insects on exhibit were huge and gorgeous. People would say to themselves, "What colors—amazing!" and plod on through the drizzle. Eyed wings wide-open in wonder, shimmering blue satin, black magic— these lingered for a while floating in one's vision, until one boarded the trolley or bought a newspaper. And, just because they were together with the butterflies, a few other objects would remain in one's memory: a globe, pencils, and a monkey's skull on a pile of copybooks.

As the street blinked and ran on, there followed again a succession of ordinary shops—soap, coal, bread—with another pause at the corner where there was a small bar. The bartender, a dashing fellow in a starched collar and green sweater, was deft at shaving off with one stroke the foam topping the glass under the beer tap; he also had a well-earned reputation as a wit. Every night, at a round table by the window, the fruiterer, the baker, an unemployed man, and the bartender's first cousin played cards with great gusto. As the winner of the current stake immediately ordered four drinks, none of the players could ever get rich.

On Saturdays, at an adjacent table, there would sit a flabby elderly man with a florid face, lank hair, and a grayish mustache, carelessly clipped. When he appeared, the players greeted him noisily without looking up from their cards. He invariably ordered rum, filled his pipe, and gazed at the game with pink-rimmed watery eyes. The left eyelid drooped slightly.

Occasionally someone turned to him, and asked how his shop was doing; he would be slow to answer, and often did not answer at all. If the bartender's daughter, a pretty freckled girl in a polka-dotted frock, happened to pass close enough, he had a go at her elusive hip, and, whether the slap succeeded or not, his gloomy expression never changed, although the veins on his temple grew purple. Mine host very humorously called him "Herr Professor." "Well, how is the Herr Professor tonight?" he would ask, coming over to him, and the man would ponder for some time in silence and then, with a wet underlip pushing out from under the pipe like that of a feeding elephant, he would answer something neither funny nor polite. The bartender would counter briskly, which made the players at the next table, though seemingly absorbed in their cards, rock with ugly glee.

The man wore a roomy gray suit with great exaggeration of the vest motif, and when the cuckoo popped out of the clock he ponderously extracted a thick silver watch and gazed at it askance, holding it in the palm of his hand and squinting because of the smoke. Punctually at eleven he knocked out his pipe, paid for his rum, and, after extending a flaccid hand to anyone who might choose to shake it, silently left.

He walked awkwardly, with a slight limp. His legs seemed too thin for his body. Just before the window of his shop he turned into a passage, where there was a door on the right with a brass plate: PAUL PILGRAM. This door led into his tiny dingy apartment, which could also be reached by an inner corridor at the back of the shop. Eleanor was usually asleep when he came home on those festive nights. Half a dozen faded photographs of the same clumsy ship, taken from different angles, and of a palm tree that looked as bleak as if it were growing on Helgoland hung in black frames above the double bed. Muttering to himself, Pilgram limped away into bulbless darkness with a lighted candle, came back with his suspenders dangling, and kept muttering while sitting on the edge of the bed and slowly, painfully, taking off his shoes. His wife, half-waking, moaned into her pillow and offered to help him; and then with a threatening rumble in his voice, he would tell her to keep quiet, and repeated that guttural *"Ruhe!"* several times, more and more fiercely.

After the stroke which had almost killed him some time ago (like a mountain falling upon him from behind just as he had bent toward his shoestrings), he now undressed reluctantly, growling until he got safely into bed, and then growling again if the faucet happened to drip in the adjoining kitchen. Eleanor would roll out of bed and totter into the kitchen and totter back with a dazed sigh, her small face wax-pale and shiny, and the plastered corns on her feet showing from under her dismally long nightgown. They had married in 1905, almost a quarter of a century before, and were childless because Pilgram had always thought that children would be merely a hindrance to the realization of what had been in his youth a delightfully exciting plan but had now gradually become a dark, passionate obsession.

He slept on his back with an old-fashioned nightcap coming down on his forehead; it was to all appearances the solid and sonorous sleep that might be expected in an elderly German shopkeeper, and one could readily suppose that his quilted torpor was entirely devoid of visions; but actually this churlish, heavy man, who fed mainly on *Erbswurst* and boiled potatoes, placidly believing in his newspaper and quite ignorant of the world (insofar as his secret passion was not involved), dreamed of things that would have seemed utterly unintelligible to his wife or his neighbors; for Pilgram belonged, or rather was meant to belong (something—the place, the time, the man— had been ill-chosen), to a special breed of dreamers, such dreamers as used to be called in the old days "Aurelians"— perhaps on account of those chrysalids, those "jewels of nature," which they loved to find hanging on fences above the dusty nettles of country lanes.

On Sundays he drank his morning coffee in several sloppy sessions, and then went out for a walk with his wife, a slow silent stroll which Eleanor looked forward to all week. On workdays he opened his shop as early as possible because of the children who passed by on their way to school; for lately he had been keeping school supplies in addition to his basic stock. Some small boy, swinging his satchel and chewing a sandwich, would slouch past the tobacconist's (where a certain brand of cigarettes offered airplane pictures), past the delicatessen (which rebuked one for having eaten that sandwich long before lunchtime), and then, remembering he wanted an eraser, would enter the next shop. Pilgram would mumble something, sticking out his lower lip from under the stem of his pipe and, after a listless search, would plump down an open carton on the counter. The boy would feel and squeeze the virgin-pale India rubber, would not find the sort he favored, and would leave without even noticing the principal wares in the store.

These modern children! Pilgram would think with disgust and he recalled his own boyhood. His father—a sailor, a rover, a bit of a rogue—married late in life a sallow-skinned, light-eyed Dutch girl whom he brought from Java to Berlin, and opened a shop of exotic curios. Pilgram could not remember now when, exactly, butterflies had begun to oust the stuffed birds of paradise, the stale talismans, the fans with dragons, and the like; but as a boy he already feverishly swapped specimens with collectors, and after his parents died butterflies reigned supreme in the dim little shop. Up to 1914 there were enough amateurs and professionals about to keep things going in a mild, very mild, way; later on, however, it became necessary to make concessions, a display case with the biography of the silkworm furnishing a transition to school supplies, just as in the old days pictures ignominiously composed of sparkling wings had probably been a first step toward lepidopterology.

Now the window contained, apart from penholders, mainly showy insects, popular stars among butterflies, some of them set on plaster and framed—intended merely for ornamenting the home. In the shop itself, permeated with the pungent odor of a disinfectant, the real, the precious collections were kept. The whole place was littered with various cases, cartons, cigar boxes. Tall cabinets contained numerous glass-lidded drawers filled with ordered series of perfect specimens impeccably spread and labeled. A dusty old shield or something (last remnant of the original wares) stood in a dark corner. Now and then live stock would appear: loaded brown pupae with a symmetrical confluence of delicate lines and grooves on the thorax, showing how the rudimentary wings, feet, antennae, and proboscis were packed. If one touched such a pupa as it lay on its bed of moss, the tapering end of the segmented abdomen would start jerking this way and that like the swathed limbs of a baby. The pupae cost a reichsmark apiece and in due time yielded a limp, bedraggled, miraculously expanding moth. And sometimes other creatures would be temporarily on sale: just then there happened to be a dozen lizards, natives of Majorca, cold, black, blue-bellied things, which Pilgram fed on mealworms for the main course and grapes for dessert.

2

He had spent all his life in Berlin and its suburbs; had never traveled farther than Peacock Island on a neighboring lake. He was a first-class entomologist. Dr. Rebel, of Vienna, had named a certain rare moth *Agrotis pilgrami;* and Pilgram himself had published several descriptions. His boxes contained most of the countries of the world, but all he had ever seen of it was the dull sand-and-pine scenery of an occasional Sunday trip; and he would be reminded of captures that had seemed to him so miraculous in his boyhood as he melancholically gazed at the familiar fauna about him, limited by a familiar landscape, to which it corresponded as hopelessly as he to his street. From a roadside shrub he would pick up a large turquoise-green caterpillar with a china-blue horn on the last ring; there it lay quite stiff on the palm of his hand, and presently, with a sigh, he would put it back on its twig as if it were some dead trinket.

Although once or twice he had had the chance to switch to a more profitable business—selling cloth, for instance, instead of moths—he stubbornly held on to his shop as the symbolic link between his dreary existence and the phantom of perfect happiness. What he craved for, with a fierce, almost morbid intensity, was *himself* to net the rarest butterflies of distant countries, to see them in flight with his own eyes, to stand waist-deep in lush grass and feel the follow-through of the swishing net and then the furious throbbing of wings through a clutched fold of the gauze.

Every year it seemed to him stranger that the year before he had not managed somehow to lay aside enough money for at least a fortnight's collecting trip abroad, but he had never been thrifty, business had always been slack, there was always a gap somewhere, and, even if luck did come his way now and then, something was sure to go wrong at the last moment. He had married counting heavily on a share in his father-in-law's business, but a month later the man had died, leaving nothing but debts. Just before World War I an unexpected deal brought a journey to Algeria so near that he even acquired a sun helmet. When all travel stopped, he still consoled himself with the hope that he might be sent to some exciting place as a soldier; but he was clumsy, sickly, not very young, and thus saw neither active service nor exotic lepidoptera. Then, after the war, when he had managed again to save a little money (for a week in Zermatt, this time), the inflation suddenly turned his meager hoard into something less than the price of a trolley-car ticket.

After that he gave up trying. He grew more and more depressed as his passion grew stronger. When some entomological acquaintance happened to drop in, Pilgram was only annoyed. That fellow, he would think, may be as learned as the late Dr. Staudinger, but he has no more imagination than a stamp collector. The glass-lidded trays over which both were bending gradually took up the whole counter, and the pipe in Pilgram's sucking lips kept emitting a wistful squeak. Pensively he gazed at the serried rows of delicate insects, all alike to you or me, and now and then he tapped on the glass with a stubby forefinger, stressing some special rarity. "That's a curiously dark aberration," the learned visitor might say. "Eisner got one like that at an auction in London, but it was not so dark, and it cost him fourteen pounds." Painfully sniffling with his extinguished pipe, Pilgram would raise the box to the light, which made the shadows of the butterflies slip from beneath them across the papered bottom; then he would put it down again and, working in his nails under the tight edges of the lid, would shake it loose with a jerk and smoothly remove it. "And Eisner's female was not so fresh," the visitor would add, and some eavesdroppers coming in for a copybook or a postage stamp might well wonder what on earth these two were talking about.

Grunting, Pilgram plucked at the gilded head of the black pin upon which the silky little creature was crucified, and took the specimen out of the box. Turning it this way and that, he peered at the label pinned under the body. "Yes— 'Tatsienlu, East Tibet,'" he read. "'Taken by the native collectors of Father Dejean'" (which sounded almost like "Prester John")—and he would stick the butterfly back again, right into the same pinhole. His motions seemed casual, even careless, but this was the unerring nonchalance of the specialist: the pin, with the precious insect, and Pilgram's fat fingers were the correlated parts of one and the same flawless machine. It might happen, however, that some open box, having been brushed by the elbow of the visitor, would stealthily begin to slide off the counter—to be stopped just in the nick of time by Pilgram, who would then calmly go on lighting his pipe; only much later, when busy elsewhere, he would suddenly produce a moan of retrospective anguish.

But not only averted crashes made him moan. Father Dejean, stout-hearted missionary climbing among the rhododendrons and snows, how enviable was thy lot! And Pilgram would stare at his boxes and puff and brood and reflect that he need not go so far: that there were thousands of hunting grounds all over Europe. Out of localities cited in entomological works he had built up a special world of his own, to which his science was a most detailed guidebook. In that world there were no casinos, no old churches, nothing that might attract a normal tourist. Digne in southern France, Ragusa in Dalmatia, Sarepta on the Volga, Abisko in Lapland—those were the famous sites dear to butterfly collectors, and this is where they had poked about, on and off, since the fifties of the last century (always greatly perplexing the local inhabitants). And as clearly as if it were a reminiscence Pilgram saw himself troubling the sleep of a little hotel by stamping and jumping about a room through the wide-open window of which, out of the black generous night, a whitish moth had dashed in and, in an audible bob dance, was kissing its shadow all over the ceiling.

In these impossible dreams of his he visited the Islands of the Blessed, where in the hot ravines that cut the lower slopes of the chestnut- and laurel-clad mountains there occurs a weird local race of the cabbage white; and also that other island, those railway banks near Vizzavona and the pine woods farther up, which are the haunts of the squat and dusky Corsican swallowtail. He visited the far North, the arctic bogs that produced such delicate downy butterflies. He knew the high alpine pastures, with those flat stones lying here and there among the slippery matted grass; for there is no greater delight than to lift such a stone and find beneath it a plump sleepy moth of a still undescribed species. He saw glazed Apollo butterflies, ocellated with red, float in the mountain draft across the mule track that ran between a steep cliff and an abyss of wild white waters. In Italian gardens in the summer dusk, the gravel crunched invitingly underfoot, and Pilgram gazed through the growing darkness at clusters of blossoms in front of which suddenly there appeared an oleander hawk, which passed from flower to flower, humming intently and stopping at the corolla, its wings vibrating so rapidly that nothing but a ghostly nimbus was visible about its streamlined body. And best of all, perhaps, were the white heathered hills near Madrid, the valleys of Andalusia, fertile and wooded Albarracin, whither a little bus driven by the forest guard's brother groaned up a twisted road.

He had more difficulty in imagining the tropics, but experienced still keener pangs when he did, for never would he catch the loftily flapping Brazilian morphos, so ample and radiant that they cast an azure reflection upon one's hand, never come upon those crowds of African butterflies closely stuck like innumerable fancy flags into the rich black mud and rising in a colored cloud when his shadow approached— a long, very long, shadow.

3

"Ja, ja, ja," he would mutter, nodding his heavy head, and holding the case before him as if it were a beloved portrait. The bell over the door would tinkle, his wife would come in with a wet umbrella and a shopping bag, and slowly he would turn his back to her as he inserted the case into the cabinet. So it went on, that obsession and that despair and that nightmarish impossibility to swindle destiny, until a certain first of April, of all dates. For more than a year he had had in his keeping a cabinet devoted solely to the genus of those small clear-winged moths that mimic wasps or mosquitoes. The widow of a great authority on that particular group had given Pilgram her husband's collection to sell on commission. He hastened to tell the silly woman that he would not be able to get more than 75 marks for it, although he knew very well that, according to catalogue prices, it was worth fifty times more, so that the amateur to whom he would sell the lot for, say, a thousand marks would consider it a good bargain. The amateur, however, did not appear, though Pilgram had written to all the wealthiest collectors. So he had locked up the cabinet, and stopped thinking about it.

That April morning a sunburned, bespectacled man in an old mackintosh and without any hat on his brown bald head sauntered in, and asked for some carbon paper. Pilgram slipped the small coins paid for the sticky violet stuff he so hated to handle into the slit of a small clay money pot and, sucking on his pipe, fixed his stare into space. The man cast a rapid glance round the shop, and remarked upon the extravagant brilliancy of an iridescent green insect with many tails. Pilgram mumbled something about Madagascar. "And that—

that's not a butterfly, is it?" said the man, indicating another specimen. Pilgram slowly replied that he had a whole collection of that special kind. *"Ach, was!"* said the man. Pilgram scratched his bristly chin, and limped into a recess of the shop. He pulled out a glass-topped tray, and laid it on the counter. The man pored over those tiny vitreous creatures with bright orange feet and belted bodies. Pilgram pointed with the stem of his pipe to one of the rows, and simultaneously the man exclaimed: "Good God—*uralensis!*" and that ejaculation gave him away. Pilgram heaped case after case on the counter as it dawned upon him that the visitor knew perfectly well of the existence of this collection, had come for its sake, was as a matter of fact the rich amateur Sommer, to whom he had written and who had just returned from a trip to Venezuela; and finally, when the question was carelessly put—"Well, and what would the price be?"—Pilgram smiled.

He knew it was madness; he knew he was leaving a helpless Eleanor, debts, unpaid taxes, a store at which only trash was bought; he knew that the 950 marks he might get would permit him to travel for no longer than a few months; and still he accepted it all as a man who felt that tomorrow would bring dreary old age and that the good fortune which now beckoned would never again repeat its invitation.

When finally Sommer said that on the fourth he would give a definite answer, Pilgram decided that the dream of his life was about to break at last from its old crinkly cocoon. He spent several hours examining a map, choosing a route, estimating the time of appearance of this or that species, and suddenly something black and blinding welled before his eyes, and he stumbled about his shop for quite a while before he felt better. The fourth came and Sommer failed to turn up, and, after waiting all day, Pilgram retired to his bedroom and silently lay down. He refused his supper, and for several minutes, with his eyes closed, nagged his wife, thinking she was still standing near; then he heard her sobbing softly in the kitchen, and toyed with the idea of taking an axe and splitting her pale-haired head. Next day he stayed in bed, and Eleanor took his place in the shop and sold a box of watercolors. And after still another day, when the whole thing seemed merely delirium, Sommer, a carnation in his buttonhole and his mackintosh on his arm, entered the store. And when he took out a wad, and the banknotes rustled, Pilgram's nose began to bleed violently.

The delivery of the cabinet and a visit to the credulous old woman, to whom he reluctantly gave 50 marks, were his last business in town. The much more expensive visit to the travel agency already referred to his new existence, where only butterflies mattered. Eleanor, though not familiar with her husband's transactions, looked happy, feeling that he had made a good profit, but fearing to ask how much. That afternoon a neighbor dropped in to remind them that tomorrow was the wedding of his daughter. So next morning Eleanor busied herself with brightening up her silk dress and pressing her husband's best suit. She would go there about five, she thought, and he would follow later, after closing time. When he looked up at her with a puzzled frown and then flatly refused to go, it did not surprise her, for she had long become used to all sorts of disappointments. "There might be champagne," she said, when already standing in the doorway. No answer—only the shuffling of boxes. She looked thoughtfully at the nice clean gloves on her hands, and went out.

Pilgram, having put the more valuable collections in order, looked at his watch and saw it was time to pack: his train left at 8:29. He locked the shop, dragged out of the corridor his father's old checkered suitcase, and packed the hunting implements first: a folding net, killing jars, pillboxes, a lantern for mothing at night on the sierras, and a few packages of pins. As an afterthought he put in a couple of spreading boards and a cork-bottomed box, though in general he intended to keep his captures in papers, as is usually done when going from place to place. Then he took the suitcase into the bedroom and threw in some thick socks and underwear. He added two or three things that might be sold in an extremity, such as, for instance, a silver tumbler and a bronze medal in a velvet case, which had belonged to his father-in-law.

Again he looked at his watch, and then decided it was time to start for the station. "Eleanor!" he called loudly, getting into his overcoat. As she did not reply, he looked into the kitchen. No, she was not there; and then vaguely he remembered something about a wedding. Hurriedly he got a scrap of paper and scribbled a few words in pencil. He left the note and the keys in a conspicuous place, and with a chill of excitement, a sinking feeling in the pit of the stomach, verified for the last time whether the money and tickets were in his wallet. *"Also los!"* said Pilgram, and gripped the suitcase.

But, as it was his first journey, he still kept worrying nervously whether there was anything he might have forgotten; then it occurred to him that he had no small change, and he remembered the clay money pot where there might be a few coins. Groaning and knocking the heavy suitcase against corners, he returned to his counter. In the twilight of the strangely still shop, eyed wings stared at him from all sides, and Pilgram perceived something almost appalling in the richness of the huge happiness that was leaning toward him like a mountain. Trying to avoid the knowing looks of those numberless eyes, he drew a deep breath and, catching sight of the hazy money pot, which seemed to hang in midair, reached quickly for it. The pot slipped from his moist grasp and broke on the floor with a dizzy spinning of twinkling coins; and Pilgram bent low to pick them up.

4

Night came; a slippery polished moon sped, without the least friction, in between chinchilla clouds, and Eleanor, returning from the wedding supper, and still all atingle from the wine and the juicy jokes, recalled her own wedding day as she leisurely walked home. Somehow all the thoughts now passing through her brain kept turning so as to show their moon-bright, attractive side; she felt almost lighthearted as she entered the gateway and proceeded to open the door, and she caught herself thinking that it was surely a great thing to have an apartment of one's own, stuffy and dark though it might be. Smiling, she turned on the light in her bedroom, and saw at once that all the drawers had been pulled open: she hardly had time to imagine burglars, for there were those keys on the night table and a bit of paper propped against the alarm clock. The note was brief: *"Off to Spain. Don't touch anything till I write. Borrow from Sch. or W. Feed the lizards."*

The faucet was dripping in the kitchen. Unconsciously she picked up her silver bag where she had dropped it, and kept on sitting on the edge of the bed, quite straight and still, with her hands in her lap as if she were having her photograph taken. After a time someone got up, walked across the room, inspected the bolted window, came back again, while she watched with indifference, not realizing that it was she who was moving. The drops of water plopped in slow succession, and suddenly she felt terrified at being alone in the house. The man whom she had loved for his mute omniscience, stolid coarseness, grim perseverance in work, had stolen away. . . . She felt like howling, running to the police, showing her marriage certificate, insisting, pleading; but still she kept on sitting, her hair slightly ruffled, her hands in white gloves.

Yes, Pilgram had gone far, very far. Most probably he visited Granada and Murcia and Albarracin, and then traveled farther still, to Surinam or Taprobane; and one can hardly doubt that he saw all the glorious bugs he had longed to see—velvety black butterflies soaring over the jungles, and a tiny moth in Tasmania, and that Chinese "skipper" said to smell of crushed roses when alive, and the short-clubbed beauty that a Mr. Baron had just discovered in Mexico. So, in a certain sense, it is quite irrelevant that some time later, upon wandering into the shop, Eleanor saw the checkered suitcase, and then her husband, sprawling on the floor with his back to the counter, among scattered coins, his livid face knocked out of shape by death.

Martin Martinich's tobacco shop is located in a corner building. No wonder tobacco shops have a predilection for corners, for Martin's business is booming. The window is of modest size, but well arranged. Small mirrors make the display come alive. At the bottom, amid the hollows of hilly azure velvet, nestles a motley of cigarette boxes with names couched in the glossy international dialect that serves for hotel names as well; higher up, rows of cigars grin in their lightweight boxes.

In his day Martin was a well-off landowner. He is famed in my childhood recollections for a remarkable tractor, while his son Petya and I succumbed simultaneously to Meyn Ried and scarlet fever, so that now, after fifteen years chock-full of all kinds of things, I enjoyed stopping by the tobacco shop on that lively corner where Martin sold his wares.

Since last year, moreover, we have more than reminiscences in common. Martin has a secret, and I have been made party to that secret. "So, everything as usual?" I ask in a whisper, and he, glancing over his shoulder, replies just as softly, "Yes, thank heaven, all is quiet." The secret is a quite extraordinary one. I recall how I was leaving for Paris and stayed at Martin's till evening the day before. A man's soul can be compared to a department store and his eyes to twin display windows. Judging by Martin's eyes, warm, brown tints were in fashion. Judging by those eyes, the merchandise inside his soul was of superb quality. And what a luxuriant beard, fairly glistening with robust Russian gray. And his shoulders, his stature, his mien. . . . At one time they used to say he could slit a handkerchief with a sword—one of the exploits of Richard Coeur de Lion. Now a fellow émigré would say with envy, "The man did not give in!"

His wife was a puffy, gentle old woman with a mole by her left nostril. Ever since the time of revolutionary ordeals her face had had a touching tic: she would give quick sidewise glances skyward. Petya had the same imposing physique as his father. I was fond of his mild-mannered glumness and unexpected humor. He had a large, flaccid face (about which his father used to say, "What a mug—three days would not suffice to circumnavigate it") and reddish-brown, permanently tousled hair. Petya owned a tiny cinema in a sparsely populated part of town, which brought a very modest income. And there we have the whole family.

I spent that day before my departure sitting by the counter and watching Martin receive his customers—first he would lean lightly, with two fingers, on the countertop, then step to the shelves, produce a box with a flourish, and ask, as he opened it with his thumbnail, *"Einen Rauchen?"*—I remember that day for a special reason: Petya suddenly came in from the street, disheveled and livid with rage. Martin's niece had decided to return to her mother in Moscow, and Petya had just been to see the diplomatic representatives. While one of the representatives was giving him some information, another, who was obviously involved with the government political directorate, whispered barely audibly, "All kinds of White Guard scum keep hanging around."

"I could have made mincemeat of him," said Petya, slamming his fist into his palm, "but unfortunately I could not forget about my aunt in Moscow."

"You already have a peccadillo or two on your conscience," good-naturedly rumbled Martin. He was alluding to a most amusing incident. Not long ago, on his nameday, Petya had visited the Soviet bookstore, whose presence blemishes one of Berlin's most charming streets. They sell not only books there, but also various handmade bric-a-brac. Petya selected a hammer adorned with poppies and emblazoned with an inscription typical for a Bolshevik hammer. The clerk inquired if he would like something else. Petya said, "Yes, I would," nodding at a small plaster bust of Mister Ulyanov.* He paid fifteen marks for bust and hammer, whereupon, without a word, right there on the counter, he popped that bust with that hammer, and with such force that Mister Ulyanov disintegrated.

I was fond of that story, just as I was fond, for instance, of the dear silly sayings from unforgettable childhood that warm the cockles of one's heart. Martin's words made me glance with a laugh at Petya. But Petya jerked his shoulder sullenly and scowled. Martin rummaged in the drawer and proffered him the most expensive cigarette in the shop. But even this did not dispel Petya's gloom.

I returned to Berlin a half-year later. One Sunday morning I felt an urge to see Martin. On weekdays you could get through via the shop, since his apartment—three rooms and kitchen—was directly behind it. But of course on a Sunday

---

*Lenin's real name. —D.N.

morning the shop was closed, and the window had shut its grated visor. I glanced rapidly through the grating at the red and gold boxes, at the swarthy cigars, at the modest inscription in a corner: "Russian spoken here," remarked that the display had in some way grown even gayer, and walked through the courtyard to Martin's place. Strange thing—Martin himself appeared to me even jollier, jauntier, more radiant than before. And Petya was downright unrecognizable: his oily, shaggy locks were combed back, a broad, vaguely bashful smile did not leave his lips, he kept a kind of sated silence, and a curious, joyous preoccupation, as if he carried a precious cargo within him, softened his every movement. Only the mother was pale as ever, and the same touching tic flashed across her face like faint summer lightning. We sat in their neat parlor, and I knew that the other two rooms—Petya's bedroom and that of his parents—were just as cozy and clean, and I found that an agreeable thought. I sipped tea with lemon, listened to Martin's mellifluous speech, and I could not rid myself of the impression that something new had appeared in their apartment, some kind of joyous, mysterious palpitation, as happens, for instance, in a home where there is a young mother-to-be. Once or twice Martin glanced with a preoccupied air at his son, whereupon the other would promptly rise, leave the room, and, on his return, nod discreetly toward his father, as if to say everything was going splendidly.

There was also something new and, to me, enigmatic in the old man's conversation. We were talking about Paris and the French, and suddenly he inquired, "Tell me, my friend, what's the largest prison in Paris?" I replied I didn't know and started telling him about a French revue that featured blue-painted women.

"You think that's something!" interrupted Martin. "They say, for example, that women scratch the plaster off the walls in prison and use it to powder their faces, necks, or whatever." In confirmation of his words he fetched from his bedroom a thick tome by a German criminologist and located in it a chapter about the routine of prison life. I tried changing the subject, but, no matter what theme I selected, Martin steered it with artful convolutions so that suddenly we would find ourselves discussing the humaneness of life imprisonment as opposed to execution, or the ingenious methods invented by criminals to break out into the free world.

I was puzzled. Petya, who loved anything mechanical, was picking with a penknife at the springs of his watch and chuckling to himself. His mother worked at her needlepoint, now and then nudging the toast or the jam toward me. Martin, clutching his disheveled beard with all five fingers, gave me a sidelong flash of his tawny eye, and suddenly something within him let go. He banged the palm of his hand on the table and turned to his son. "I can't stand it any longer, Petya—I'm going to tell him everything before I burst." Petya nodded silently. Martin's wife was getting up to go to the kitchen. "What a chatterbox you are," she said, shaking her head indulgently. Martin placed his hand on my shoulder, gave me such a shake that, had I been an apple tree in the garden, the apples would literally have come tumbling off me, and glanced into my face. "I'm warning you," he said. "I'm about to tell you such a secret, such a secret . . . that I just don't know. Mind you—mum's the word! Understand?"

And, leaning close to me, bathing me in the odor of tobacco and his own pungent old-man smell, Martin told me a truly remarkable tale.*

---

*In this narrative, all traits and distinguishing marks that might hint at the identity of the real Martin are of course deliberately distorted. I mention this so that curiosity seekers will not search in vain for the "tobacco shop in the corner building."—V.N.

"It happened," began Martin, "shortly after your departure. In walked a customer. He had obviously not noticed the sign in the window, for he addressed me in German. Let me emphasize this: if he had noticed the sign he would not have entered a modest émigré shop. I recognized him right off as a Russian by his pronunciation. Had a Russian mug too. I, of course, launched into Russian, asked him what price range, what kind. He gave me a look of disagreeable surprise: 'What made you think I was Russian?' I gave him a perfectly friendly answer, as I recall, and began counting out his cigarettes. At that moment Petya entered. When he saw my customer he said with utter calm, 'Now here's a pleasant encounter.' Then my Petya walks up close to him and bangs him on the cheek with his fist. The other froze. As Petya explained to me later, what had happened was not just a knockout with the victim crumpling to the floor, but a special kind of knockout: it turns out Petya had delivered a delayed-action punch, and the man went out on his feet. And looked as if he were sleeping standing up. Then he started slowly tilting back like a tower. Here Petya walked around behind him and caught him under the armpits. It was all highly unexpected. Petya said, 'Give me a hand, Dad.' I asked what he thought he was doing. Petya only repeated, 'Give me a hand.' I know my Petya well—no point in smirking, Petya—and know he has his feet on the ground, ponders his actions, and does not knock people unconscious for nothing. We dragged the unconscious one from the shop into the corridor and on to Petya's room. Right then I heard a ring—someone had stepped into the shop. Good thing, of course, that it hadn't happened earlier. Back into the shop I went, made my sale, then, luckily, my wife arrived with the shopping, and I immediately put her to work at the counter while I, without a word, went lickety-split into Petya's room. The man was lying with eyes closed

on the floor, while Petya was sitting at his table, examining in
a pensive kind of way certain objects like that large leather
cigar case, half a dozen obscene postcards, a wallet, a passport,
an old but apparently efficient revolver. He explained right
away: as I'm sure you have imagined, these items came from
the man's pockets, and the man himself was none other than
the representative—you remember Petya's story—who made
the crack about the White scum, yes, yes, the very same one!
And, judging by certain papers, he was a GPU man if I ever
saw one. 'Well and good,' I say to Petya, 'so you've punched
a guy in the mug. Whether he deserved it or not is a different
matter, but please explain to me, what do you intend to do
now? Evidently you forgot all about your aunt in Moscow.'
'Yes, I did,' said Petya. 'We must think of something.'

"And we did. First we got hold of some stout rope, and
plugged his mouth with a towel. While we were working on
him he came to and opened one eye. Upon closer examination, let me tell you, the mug turned out to be not only
repulsive but stupid as well—some kind of mange on his
forehead, mustache, bulbous nose. Leaving him lying on the
floor, Petya and I settled down comfortably nearby and
started a judicial inquiry. We debated for a good while. We
were concerned not so much with the affront itself—that was
a trifle, of course—as much as with his entire profession, so
to speak, and with the deeds he had committed in Russia.
The defendant was allowed to have the last word. When we
relieved his mouth of the towel, he gave a kind of moan,
gagged, but said nothing except 'You wait, you just wait. . . .'
The towel was retied, and the session resumed. The votes
were split at first. Petya demanded the death sentence. I found
that he deserved to die, but proposed substituting life imprisonment for execution. Petya thought it over and concurred. I
added that although he had certainly committed crimes, we

were unable to ascertain this; that his employment in itself alone constituted a crime; that our duty was limited to rendering him harmless, nothing more. Now listen to the rest.

"We have a bathroom at the end of the corridor. Dark, very dark little room, with an enameled iron bathtub. The water goes on strike pretty often. There is an occasional cockroach. The room is so dark because the window is extremely narrow and is situated right under the ceiling, and besides, right opposite the window, three feet away or less, there's a good, solid brick wall. And it was here in this nook that we decided to keep the prisoner. It was Petya's idea—yes, yes, Petya, give Caesar his due. First of all, of course, the cell had to be prepared. We began by dragging the prisoner into the corridor so he would be close by while we worked. And here my wife, who had just locked up the shop for the night and was on her way to the kitchen, saw us. She was amazed, even indignant, but then understood our reasoning. Docile girl. Petya began by dismembering a stout table we had in the kitchen—knocked off its legs and used the resulting board to hammer shut the bathroom window. Then he unscrewed the taps, removed the cylindrical water heater, and laid a mattress on the bathroom floor. Of course next day we added various improvements: we changed the lock, installed a deadbolt, reinforced the window board with metal—and all of it, of course, without making too much noise. As you know, we have no neighbors, but nonetheless it behooved us to act cautiously. The result was a real prison cell, and there we put the GPU chap. We undid the rope, untied the towel, warned him that if he started yelling we would reswaddle him, and for a long time; then, satisfied that he had understood for whom the mattress had been placed in the bathtub, we locked the door and, taking turns, stood guard all night.

"That moment marked the beginning of a new life for us.

I was no longer simply Martin Martinich, but Martin Martinich the head warden. At first the inmate was so stunned by
what had happened that his behavior was subdued. Soon,
however, he reverted to a normal state and, when we brought
his dinner, launched into a hurricane of foul language. I cannot repeat the man's obscenities; I shall limit myself to saying
that he placed my dear late mother in the most curious situations. It was decided to inculcate in him thoroughly the
nature of his legal status. I explained that he would remain
imprisoned until the end of his days; that if I died first I
would transmit him to Petya like a bequest; that my son in his
turn would transmit him to my future grandson and so forth,
causing him to become a kind of family tradition. A family
jewel. I mentioned in passing that, in the unlikely eventuality
of our having to move to a different Berlin flat, he would be
tied up, placed in a special trunk, and would make the move
with us easy as pie. I went on to explain to him that in one
case only would he be granted amnesty. Namely, he would be
released the day the Bolshevik bubble burst. Finally I promised that he would be well fed—far better than when, in my
time, I had been locked up by the Cheka—and that, by way
of special privilege, he would receive books. And in fact, to
this day I don't believe he has once complained about the
food. True, at first Petya proposed that he be fed dried roach,
but search as he might, that Soviet fish was unavailable in
Berlin. We are obliged to give him bourgeois food. Exactly at
eight every morning Petya and I go in and place by his tub a
bowl of hot soup with meat and a loaf of gray bread. At the
same time we take out the chamber pot, a clever apparatus we
acquired just for him. At three he gets a glass of tea, at seven
some more soup. This nutritional system is modeled on the
one in use in the best European jails.

"The books were more of a problem. We held a family

council for starters, and stopped at three titles: *Prince Sere-bryaniÿ,* Krylov's *Fables,* and *Around the World in Eighty Days.* He announced that he would not read those 'White Guard pamphlets,' but we left him the books, and we have every reason to believe that he read them with pleasure.

"His mood was changeable. He grew quiet. Evidently he was cooking up something. Maybe he hoped the police would start looking for him. We checked the papers, but there was not a word about the vanished Cheka agent. Most likely the other representatives had decided the man had simply defected, and had preferred to bury the affair. To this pensive period belongs his attempt to slip away, or at least to get word to the outside world. He trudged about his cell, probably reached for the window, tried to pry the planks loose, tried pounding, but we made some threat or other and the pounding ceased. And once, when Petya went in there alone, the man lunged at him. Petya grabbed him in a gentle bear hug and sat him back in the tub. After this occurrence he underwent another change, became very good-natured, even joked on occasion, and finally attempted to bribe us. He offered us an enormous sum, promising to obtain it through somebody. When this did not help either, he started whimpering, then went back to swearing worse than before. At the moment he is at a stage of grim submissiveness, which, I'm afraid, bodes no good.

"We take him for a daily walk in the corridor, and twice a week we air him out by an open window; naturally we take all necessary precautions to prevent him from yelling. On Saturdays he takes a bath. We ourselves have to wash in the kitchen. On Sundays I give him short lectures and let him smoke three cigarettes—in my presence, of course. What are these lectures about? All sorts of things. Pushkin, for instance, or Ancient Greece. Only one subject is omitted—politics. He is totally deprived of politics. Just as if such a thing did not exist on the face of the earth. And you know what? Ever since I have kept one Soviet agent locked up, ever since I have served the Fatherland, I am simply a different man. Jaunty and happy. And business has looked up, so there is no great problem supporting him either. He costs me twenty marks or so a month, counting the electric bill: it's completely dark in there, so from eight A.M. to eight P.M. one weak lightbulb is left on.

"You ask, what milieu is he from? Well, how shall I put it. . . . He is twenty-four years old, he is a peasant, it is unlikely that he finished even a village school, he was what is called 'an honest Communist,' studied only political literacy, which in our book signifies trying to make blockheads out of knuckleheads—that's all I know. Oh, if you want I'll show him to you, only remember, mum's the word!"

Martin went into the corridor. Petya and I followed. The old man in his cozy house jacket really did look like a prison warden. He produced the key as he walked, and there was something almost professional in the way he inserted it in the lock. The lock crunched twice, and Martin threw open the door. Far from being some ill-lit hole, it was a splendid, spacious bathroom, of the kind one finds in comfortable German dwellings. Electric light, bright yet pleasing to the eye, burned behind a merry, ornate shade. A mirror glistened on the left-hand wall. On the night table by the bathtub there were books, a peeled orange on a lustrous plate, and an untouched bottle of beer. In the white bathtub, on a mattress covered with a clean sheet, with a large pillow under the back of his head, lay a well-fed, bright-eyed fellow with a long growth of beard, in a bathrobe (a hand-me-down from the master) and warm, soft slippers.

"Well, what do you say?" Martin asked me.

I found the scene comical and did not know what to answer. "That's where the window used to be," Martin indicated with his finger. Sure enough, the window was boarded up to perfection.

The prisoner yawned and turned toward the wall. We went out. Martin fondled the bolt with a smile. "Fat chance he'll ever escape," he said, and then added pensively, "I would be curious to know, though, just how many years he'll spend in there. . . ."

CLOUD, CASTLE, LAKE

One of my representatives—a modest, mild bachelor, very efficient—happened to win a pleasure trip at a charity ball given by Russian refugees. That was in 1936 or 1937. The Berlin summer was in full flood (it was the second week of damp and cold, so that it was a pity to look at everything which had turned green in vain, and only the sparrows kept cheerful); he did not care to go anywhere, but when he tried to sell his ticket at the office of the Bureau of Pleasantrips he was told that to do so he would have to have special permission from the Ministry of Transportation; when he tried them, it turned out that first he would have to draw up a complicated petition at a notary's on stamped paper; and besides, a so-called "certificate of nonabsence from the city for the summertime" had to be obtained from the police.

So he sighed a little, and decided to go. He borrowed an aluminum flask from friends, repaired his soles, bought a belt and a fancy-style flannel shirt—one of those cowardly things which shrink in the first wash. Incidentally, it was too large for that likable little man, his hair always neatly trimmed, his eyes so intelligent and kind. I cannot remember his name at the moment. I think it was Vasiliy Ivanovich.

He slept badly the night before the departure. And why? Because he had to get up unusually early, and hence took along into his dreams the delicate face of the watch ticking on his night table; but mainly because that very night, for no reason at all, he began to imagine that this trip, thrust upon him by a feminine fate in a low-cut gown, this trip which he had accepted so reluctantly, would bring him some wonderful, tremulous happiness. This happiness would have something in common with his childhood, and with the excitement aroused in him by Russian lyrical poetry, and with some evening skyline once seen in a dream, and with that lady, another man's wife, whom he had hopelessly loved for seven years—but it would be even fuller and more significant than all that. And besides, he felt that the really good life must be oriented toward something or someone.

The morning was dull, but steam-warm and close, with an inner sun, and it was quite pleasant to rattle in a streetcar to the distant railway station where the gathering place was: several people, alas, were taking part in the excursion. Who would they be, these drowsy beings, drowsy as seem all creatures still unknown to us? By Window Number 6, at seven A.M., as was indicated in the directions appended to the ticket, he saw them (they were already waiting; he had managed to be late by about three minutes).

A lanky blond young man in Tyrolese garb stood out at once. He was burned the color of a cockscomb, had huge brick-red knees with golden hairs, and his nose looked lacquered. He was the leader furnished by the Bureau, and as soon as the newcomer had joined the group (which consisted of four women and as many men) he led it off toward a train lurking behind other trains, carrying his monstrous knapsack with terrifying ease, and firmly clanking with his hobnailed boots.

Everyone found a place in an empty car, unmistakably

third-class, and Vasiliy Ivanovich, having sat down by himself
and put a peppermint into his mouth, opened a little volume
of Tyutchev, whom he had long intended to reread; but he
was requested to put the book aside and join the group. An
elderly bespectacled post-office clerk, with skull, chin, and
upper lip a bristly blue as if he had shaved off some extraordi-
narily luxuriant and tough growth especially for this trip,
immediately announced that he had been to Russia and knew
some Russian—for instance, *patzlui*—and, recalling philan-
derings in Tsaritsyn, winked in such a manner that his fat wife
sketched out in the air the outline of a backhand box on the
ear. The company was getting noisy. Four employees of the
same building firm were tossing each other heavy-weight
jokes: a middle-aged man, Schultz; a younger man, Schultz
also, and two fidgety young women with big mouths and big
rumps. The redheaded, rather burlesque widow in a sport skirt
knew something too about Russia (the Riga beaches). There
was also a dark young man by the name of Schramm, with
lusterless eyes and a vague velvety vileness about his person
and manners, who constantly switched the conversation to
this or that attractive aspect of the excursion, and who gave
the first signal for rapturous appreciation; he was, as it turned
out later, a special stimulator from the Bureau of Pleasantrips.

The locomotive, working rapidly with its elbows, hurried
through a pine forest, then—with relief—among fields. Only
dimly realizing as yet all the absurdity and horror of the situation, and perhaps attempting to persuade himself that everything was very nice, Vasiliy Ivanovich contrived to enjoy the
fleeting gifts of the road. And indeed, how enticing it all is,
what charm the world acquires when it is wound up and
moving like a merry-go-round! The sun crept toward a corner of the window and suddenly spilled over the yellow bench.
The badly pressed shadow of the car sped madly along the

grassy bank, where flowers blended into colored streaks. A crossing: a cyclist was waiting, one foot resting on the ground. Trees appeared in groups and singly, revolving coolly and blandly, displaying the latest fashions. The blue dampness of a ravine. A memory of love, disguised as a meadow. Wispy clouds—greyhounds of heaven.

We both, Vasiliy Ivanovich and I, have always been impressed by the anonymity of all the parts of a landscape, so dangerous for the soul, the impossibility of ever finding out where that path you see leads—and look, what a tempting thicket! It happened that on a distant slope or in a gap in the trees there would appear and, as it were, stop for an instant, like air retained in the lungs, a spot so enchanting—a lawn, a terrace—such perfect expression of tender well-meaning beauty—that it seemed that if one could stop the train and go thither, for-ever, to you, my love. . . . But a thousand beech trunks were already madly leaping by, whirling in a sizzling sun pool, and again the chance for happiness was gone.

At the stations, Vasiliy Ivanovich would look at the config-uration of some entirely insignificant objects—a smear on the platform, a cherry stone, a cigarette butt—and would say to himself that never, never would he remember these three lit-tle things here in that particular interrelation, this pattern, which he now could see with such deathless precision; or again, looking at a group of children waiting for a train, he would try with all his might to single out at least one remark-able destiny—in the form of a violin or a crown, a propeller or a lyre—and would gaze until the whole party of village schoolboys appeared as in an old photograph, now repro-duced with a little white cross above the face of the last boy on the right: the hero's childhood.

But one could look out of the window only by snatches. All had been given sheet music with verses from the Bureau:

Stop that worrying and moping,
Take a knotted stick and rise,
Come a-tramping in the open
With the good, the hearty guys!

Tramp your country's grass and stubble,
With the good, the hearty guys,
Kill the hermit and his trouble
And to hell with doubts and sighs!

In a paradise of heather
Where the field mouse screams and dies,
Let us march and sweat together
With the steel-and-leather guys!

This was to be sung in chorus: Vasiliy Ivanovich, who not only could not sing but could not even pronounce German words clearly, took advantage of the drowning roar of mingling voices and merely opened his mouth while swaying slightly, as if he were really singing—but the leader, at a sign from the subtle Schramm, suddenly stopped the general singing and, squinting askance at Vasiliy Ivanovich, demanded that he sing solo. Vasiliy Ivanovich cleared his throat, timidly began, and after a minute of solitary torment all joined in; but he did not dare thereafter to drop out.

He had with him his favorite cucumber from the Russian store, a loaf of bread, and three eggs. When evening came, and the low crimson sun entered wholly the soiled seasick car, stunned by its own din, all were invited to hand over their provisions, in order to divide them evenly—this was particularly easy, as all except Vasiliy Ivanovich had the same things. The cucumber amused everybody, was pronounced inedible, and was thrown out of the window. In view of the insufficiency of his contribution, Vasiliy Ivanovich got a smaller portion of sausage.

He was made to play cards. They pulled him about, questioned him, verified whether he could show the route of the trip on a map—in a word, all busied themselves with him, at first good-naturedly, then with malevolence, which grew with the approach of night. Both girls were called Greta; the red-headed widow somehow resembled the rooster-leader; Schramm, Schultz, and the other Schultz, the post-office clerk and his wife, all gradually melted together, merged together, forming one collective, wobbly, many-handed being, from which one could not escape. It pressed upon him from all sides. But suddenly at some station all climbed out, and it was already dark, although in the west there still hung a very long, very pink cloud, and farther along the track, with a soul-piercing light, the star of a lamp trembled through the slow smoke of the engine, and crickets chirped in the dark, and from somewhere there came the odor of jasmine and hay, my love.

They spent the night in a tumble-down inn. A mature bedbug is awful, but there is a certain grace in the motions of silky silverfish. The post-office clerk was separated from his wife, who was put with the widow; he was given to Vasiliy Ivanovich for the night. The two beds took up the whole room. Quilt on top, chamber pot below. The clerk said that somehow he did not feel sleepy, and began to talk of his Russian adventures, rather more circumstantially than in the train. He was a great bully of a man, thorough and obstinate, clad in long cotton drawers, with mother-of-pearl claws on his dirty toes, and bear's fur between fat breasts. A moth dashed about the ceiling, hobnobbing with its shadow. "In Tsaritsyn," the clerk was saying, "there are now three schools, a German, a Czech, and a Chinese one. At any rate, that is what my brother-in-law says; he went there to build tractors."

Next day, from early morning to five o'clock in the afternoon, they raised dust along a highway, which undulated from hill to hill; then they took a green road through a dense fir wood. Vasiliy Ivanovich, as the least burdened, was given an enormous round loaf of bread to carry under his arm. How I hate you, our daily! But still his precious, experienced eyes noted what was necessary. Against the background of fir-tree gloom a dry needle was hanging vertically on an invisible thread.

Again they piled into a train, and again the small partition-less car was empty. The other Schultz began to teach Vasiliy Ivanovich how to play the mandolin. There was much laughter. When they got tired of that, they thought up a capital game, which was supervised by Schramm. It consisted of the following: the women would lie down on the benches they chose, under which the men were already hidden, and when from under one of the benches there would emerge a ruddy face with ears, or a big outspread hand, with a skirt-lifting curve of the fingers (which would provoke much squealing), then it would be revealed who was paired off with whom. Three times Vasiliy Ivanovich lay down in filthy darkness, and three times it turned out that there was no one on the bench when he crawled out from under. He was acknowledged the loser and was forced to eat a cigarette butt.

They spent the night on straw mattresses in a barn, and early in the morning set out again on foot. Firs, ravines, foamy streams. From the heat, from the songs which one had constantly to bawl, Vasiliy Ivanovich became so exhausted that during the midday halt he fell asleep at once, and awoke only when they began to slap at imaginary horseflies on him. But after another hour of marching, that very happiness of which he had once half dreamt was suddenly discovered.

It was a pure, blue lake, with an unusual expression of its water. In the middle, a large cloud was reflected in its entirety. On the other side, on a hill thickly covered with verdure (and the darker the verdure, the more poetic it is), towered, arising from dactyl to dactyl, an ancient black castle. Of course, there are plenty of such views in Central Europe, but just this one—in the inexpressible and unique harmoniousness of its three principal parts, in its smile, in some mysterious innocence it had, my love! my obedient one!—was something so unique, and so familiar, and so long-promised, and it so *understood* the beholder that Vasiliy Ivanovich even pressed his hand to his heart, as if to see whether his heart was there in order to give it away.

At some distance, Schramm, poking into the air with the leader's alpenstock, was calling the attention of the excursionists to something or other; they had settled themselves around on the grass in poses seen in amateur snapshots, while the leader sat on a stump, his behind to the lake, and was having a snack. Quietly, concealing himself in his own shadow, Vasiliy Ivanovich followed the shore, and came to a kind of inn. A dog still quite young greeted him; it crept on its belly, its jaws laughing, its tail fervently beating the ground. Vasiliy Ivanovich accompanied the dog into the house, a piebald two-storied dwelling with a winking window beneath a convex tiled eyelid; and he found the owner, a tall old man vaguely resembling a Russian war veteran, who spoke German so poorly and with such a soft drawl that Vasiliy Ivanovich changed to his own tongue, but the man understood as in a dream and continued in the language of his environment, his family.

Upstairs was a room for travelers. "You know, I shall take it for the rest of my life," Vasiliy Ivanovich is reported to have said as soon as he had entered it. The room itself had nothing remarkable about it. On the contrary, it was a most ordinary room, with a red floor, daisies daubed on the white walls, and a small mirror half filled with the yellow infusion of the reflected flowers—but from the window one could clearly see the lake with its cloud and its castle, in a motionless and perfect correlation of happiness. Without reasoning, without considering, only entirely surrendering to an attraction the truth of which consisted in its own strength, a strength which he had never experienced before, Vasiliy Ivanovich in one radiant second realized that here in this little room with that view, beautiful to the verge of tears, life would at last be what he had always wished it to be. What exactly it would be like, what would take place here, that of course he did not know, but all around him were help, promise, and consolation—so that there could not be any doubt that he must live here. In a moment he figured out how he would manage it so as not to have to return to Berlin again, how to get the few possessions that he had—books, the blue suit, her photograph. How simple it was turning out! As my representative, he was earning enough for the modest life of a refugee Russian.

"My friends," he cried, having run down again to the meadow by the shore, "my friends, good-bye. I shall remain for good in that house over there. We can't travel together any longer. I shall go no farther. I am not going anywhere. Good-bye!"

"How is that?" said the leader in a queer voice, after a short pause, during which the smile on the lips of Vasiliy Ivanovich slowly faded, while the people who had been sitting on the grass half rose and stared at him with stony eyes.

"But why?" he faltered. "It is here that . . ."

"Silence!" the post-office clerk suddenly bellowed with extraordinary force. "Come to your senses, you drunken swine!"

"Wait a moment, gentlemen," said the leader, and, having passed his tongue over his lips, he turned to Vasiliy Ivanovich.

"You probably have been drinking," he said quietly. "Or have gone out of your mind. You are taking a pleasure trip with us. Tomorrow, according to the appointed itinerary— look at your ticket—we are all returning to Berlin. There can be no question of anyone—in this case you—refusing to continue this communal journey. We were singing today a certain song—try and remember what it said. That's enough now! Come, children, we are going on."

"There will be beer at Ewald," said Schramm in a caressing voice. "Five hours by train. Hikes. A hunting lodge. Coal mines. Lots of interesting things."

"I shall complain," wailed Vasiliy Ivanovich. "Give me back my bag. I have the right to remain where I want. Oh, but this is nothing less than an invitation to a beheading"—he told me he cried when they seized him by the arms.

"If necessary we shall carry you," said the leader grimly, "but that is not likely to be pleasant. I am responsible for each of you, and shall bring back each of you, alive or dead."

Swept along a forest road as in a hideous fairy tale, squeezed, twisted, Vasiliy Ivanovich could not even turn around, and only felt how the radiance behind his back receded, fractured by trees, and then it was no longer there, and all around the dark firs fretted but could not interfere. As soon as everyone had got into the car and the train had pulled off, they began to beat him—they beat him a long time, and with a good deal of inventiveness. It occurred to them, among other things, to use a corkscrew on his palms; then on his feet. The post-office clerk, who had been to Russia, fashioned a knout out of a stick and a belt, and began to use it with devilish dexterity. Atta boy! The other men relied more on their iron heels, whereas the women were satisfied to pinch and slap. All had a wonderful time.

After returning to Berlin, he called on me, was much changed, sat down quietly, putting his hands on his knees, told his story; kept on repeating that he must resign his position, begged me to let him go, insisted that he could not continue, that he had not the strength to belong to mankind any longer. Of course, I let him go.

MADEMOISELLE O

1

I have often noticed that after I had bestowed on the characters of my novels some treasured item of my past, it would pine away in the artificial world where I had so abruptly placed it. Although it lingered on in my mind, its personal warmth, its retrospective appeal had gone and, presently, it became more closely identified with my novel than with my former self, where it had seemed to be so safe from the intrusion of the artist. Houses have crumbled in my memory as soundlessly as they did in the mute films of yore; and the portrait of my old French governess, whom I once lent to a boy in one of my books, is fading fast, now that it is engulfed in the description of a childhood entirely unrelated to my own. The man in me revolts against the fictionist and here is my desperate attempt to save what is left of poor Mademoiselle.

A large woman, a very stout woman, Mademoiselle rolled into our existence in 1905 when I was six and my brother five. There she is. I see so plainly her abundant dark hair, brushed up high and covertly graying; the three wrinkles on her austere forehead; her beetling brows; the steely eyes behind the black-rimmed pince-nez; that vestigial mustache; that blotchy complexion, which in moments of wrath develops an additional

flush in the region of the third, and amplest, chin so regally
spread over the frilled mountain of her blouse. And now she
sits down, or rather she tackles the job of sitting down, the jelly
of her jowl quaking, her prodigious posterior, with the three
buttons on the side, lowering itself warily; then, at the last second, she surrenders her bulk to the wicker armchair, which
out of sheer fright bursts into a salvo of crackling.

The winter she came was the only one of my childhood
that I spent in the country. It was a year of strikes, riots, and
police-inspired massacres; and I suppose my father wished to
tuck his family away from the city, in our quiet country place,
where his popularity with the peasants might mitigate, as he
correctly surmised, the risk of agrarian troubles. It was also a
particularly severe winter, producing as much snow as Mademoiselle might have expected to find in the Hyperborean
gloom of remote Muscovy. When she alighted at the little station, from which she still had to travel half a dozen miles by
sleigh to our country home, I was not there to greet her; but
I do so now as I try to imagine what she saw and felt at that
last stage of her fabulous and ill-timed journey. Her Russian
vocabulary consisted, I know, of one short word, the same
solitary word that years later she was to take back to Switzerland, where she had been born of French parents. This word,
which in her pronunciation may be phonetically rendered as
"giddy-eh" (actually it is *gde,* with *e* as in "yet"), meant
"Where?" And that was a good deal. Uttered by her like the
raucous cry of some lost bird, it accumulated such interroga-
tory force that it sufficed for all her needs. "Giddy-eh? Giddy-
eh?" she would wail, not only to find out her whereabouts
but also to express an abyss of misery: the fact that she was a
stranger, shipwrecked, penniless, ailing, in search of the blessed
land where at last she would be understood.

I can visualize her, by proxy, as she stands in the middle of

the station platform, where she has just alighted, and vainly
my ghostly envoy offers her an arm that she cannot see. The
door of the waiting room opens with a shuddering whine
peculiar to nights of intense frost; a cloud of hot air rushes
out, almost as profuse as the steam from the great stack of the
panting engine; and now our coachman Zakhar takes over—
a burly man in sheepskin with the leather outside, his huge
gloves protruding from his scarlet sash into which he has
stuffed them. I hear the snow crunching under his felt boots
while he busies himself with the luggage, the jingling har-
ness, and then his own nose, which he eases by means of a
dexterous flip of finger and thumb as he trudges back round
the sleigh. Slowly, with grim misgivings, Mademoiselle climbs
in, clutching at her helper in mortal fear lest the sleigh move
off before her vast form is securely encased. Finally, she settles
down with a grunt and thrusts her fists into her skimpy plush
muff. At the juicy smack of their driver's lips the horses strain
their quarters, shift hooves, strain again; and then Mademoiselle gives a backward jerk of her torso as the heavy sleigh is
wrenched out of its world of steel, fur, flesh, to enter a fric-
tionless medium where it skims along a spectral road that it
seems barely to touch.

For one moment, thanks to the sudden radiance of a lone
lamp where the station square ends, a grossly exaggerated
shadow, also holding a muff, races beside the sleigh, climbs a
billow of snow, and is gone, leaving Mademoiselle to be swal-
lowed up by what she will later allude to, with awe and gusto,
as *"la steppe."* There, in the limitless gloom, the changeable
twinkle of remote village lights seems to her to be the yellow
eyes of wolves. She is cold, she is frozen stiff, frozen "to the
center of her brain," for she soars with the wildest hyperbole
when not clinging to the safest old saw. Every now and then,
she looks back to make sure that a second sleigh, bearing her

trunk and hatbox, is following—always at the same distance, like those companionable phantoms of ships in polar waters which explorers have described. And let me not leave out the moon—for surely there must be a moon, the full, incredibly clear disc that goes so well with Russian lusty frosts. So there it comes, steering out of a flock of small dappled clouds, which it tinges with a vague iridescence; and, as it sails higher, it glazes the runner tracks left on the road, where every sparkling lump of snow is emphasized by a swollen shadow.

Very lovely, very lonesome. But what am I doing there in that stereoscopic dreamland? Somehow those two sleighs have slipped away; they have left my imaginary double behind on the blue-white road. No, even the vibration in my ears is not their receding bells, but my own blood singing. All is still, spellbound, enthralled by that great heavenly O shining above the Russian wilderness of my past. The snow is real, though, and as I bend to it and scoop up a handful, forty-five years crumble to glittering frost-dust between my fingers.

2

A kerosene lamp is steered into the gloaming. Gently it floats and comes down; the hand of memory, now in a footman's white cotton glove, places it in the center of a round table. The flame is nicely adjusted, and a rosy, silk-flounced lamp shade crowns the light. Revealed: a warm, bright room in a snow-muffled house—soon to be termed *"le château"*—built by my great-grandfather, who, being afraid of fires, had the staircase made of iron, so that when the house did get burnt to the ground, sometime after the Soviet Revolution, those fretted steps remained standing there, all alone but still leading up.

Some more about that room, please. The oval mirror. Hanging on taut cords, its pure brow inclined, it strives to retain the falling furniture and a slope of bright floor that keep slipping from its embrace. The chandelier pendants. These emit a delicate tinkling whenever anything is moved in an upstairs room. Colored pencils. That tiny heap of emerald pencil dust on the oilcloth where a penknife had just done its recurrent duty. We are sitting at the table, my brother and I and Miss Robinson, who now and then looks at her watch: roads must be dreadful with all that snow; and anyway many professional hardships lie in wait for the vague French person who will replace her.

Now the colored pencils in more detail. The green one, by a mere whirl of the wrist, could be made to produce a ruffled tree, or the chimney smoke of a house where spinach was cooking. The blue one drew a simple line across the page— and the horizon of all seas was there. A nondescript blunt one kept getting into one's way. The brown one was always broken, and so was the red, but sometimes, just after it had snapped, one could still make it serve by holding it so that the loose tip was propped, none too securely, by a jutting splinter. The little purple fellow, a special favorite of mine, had got worn down so short as to become scarcely manageable. The white one alone, that lanky albino among pencils, kept its original length, or at least did so until I discovered that, far from being a fraud leaving no mark on the page, it was the ideal tool since I could imagine whatever I wished while I scrawled.

Alas, these pencils, too, have been distributed among the characters in my books to keep fictitious children busy; they are not quite my own now. Somewhere, in the apartment house of a chapter, in the hired room of a paragraph, I have also placed that tilted mirror, and the lamp, and the chandelier-drops. Few things are left; many have been squandered. Have I given away Box (son and husband of Loulou, the house-keeper's pet), that old brown dachshund fast asleep on the sofa? No, I think he is still mine. His grizzled muzzle, with the wart at the puckered corner of the mouth, is tucked into the curve of his hock, and from time to time a deep sigh dis-tends his ribs. He is so old and his sleep is so thickly padded with dreams (about chewable slippers and a few last smells) that he does not stir when faint bells jingle outside. Then a pneumatic door heaves and clangs in the vestibule. She has come after all: I had so hoped she would not.

3

Another dog, the sweet-tempered sire of a ferocious family, a Great Dane not allowed in the house, played a pleasant part in an adventure that took place on one of the following days, if not the very day after. It so happened that my brother and I were left completely in charge of the newcomer. As I recon-struct it now, my mother had probably gone for a few hours to St. Petersburg (a distance of some fifty miles) where my father was deeply involved in the grave political events of that winter. She was pregnant and very nervous. Miss Robinson, instead of staying to break in Mademoiselle, had gone too— or perhaps my little sister, aged three, had inherited her. In order to prove that this was no way of treating us, I immedi-ately formed the project of repeating the exciting perfor-mance of a year before, when we escaped from poor Miss Hunt in gay, populous Wiesbaden, a paradise of multicolored dead leaves. This time the countryside all around was a wilderness of snow, and it is hard to imagine what exactly could have been the goal of the journey I planned. We had

just returned from our first afternoon walk with Mademoiselle and were throbbing with frustration and hatred. To keep
up with an unfamiliar tongue (all we knew in the way of
French were a few household words), and on top of it to be
crossed in all our fond habits, was more than we could bear.
The *bonne promenade* she had promised us had turned out to
be a tedious stroll around the house where the snow had been
cleared and the icy ground sprinkled with sand. She had had
us wear things we never used to wear, even on the frostiest
day—horrible gaiters and hoods that hampered our every
movement. She had restrained us when we were tempted to
explore the creamy, smooth swellings of snow that had been
flower beds in summer. She had not allowed us to walk under
the organ-pipe-like system of huge icicles that hung from the
eaves and gloriously burned in the low sun. As soon as we
came back from that walk, we left Mademoiselle puffing on
the steps of the vestibule and dashed indoors, giving her the
impression that we were about to conceal ourselves in some
remote room. Actually, we trotted on till we reached the
other side of the house, and then, through a veranda,
emerged into the garden again. The above-mentioned Great
Dane was in the act of fussily adjusting himself to a nearby
snowdrift, but while deciding which hind leg to lift he
noticed us and at once joined us at a joyful gallop.

The three of us followed a fairly easy trail and, after plodding through deeper snow, reached the road that led to the
village. Meanwhile the sun had set. Dusk came with uncanny
suddenness. My brother declared he was cold and tired, but I
urged him on and finally made him ride the dog (the only
member of the party to be still enjoying himself). We had
gone more than two miles and the moon was fantastically
shiny, and my brother, in perfect silence, had begun to fall
every now and then from his mount, when a servant with a

lantern overtook us and led us home. "Giddy-eh, giddy-eh?" Mademoiselle was frantically shouting from the porch. I brushed past her without a word. My brother burst into tears, and gave himself up. The Great Dane, whose name was Turka, returned to his interrupted affairs in connection with serviceable and informative snowdrifts around the house.

4

In our childhood we know a lot about hands since they live and hover at the level of our stature; Mademoiselle's were unpleasant because of the froggy gloss on their tight skin besprinkled with brown ecchymotic spots. Before her time no stranger had ever stroked my face. Mademoiselle, as soon as she came, had taken me completely aback by patting my cheek in sign of spontaneous affection. All her mannerisms come back to me when I think of her hands. Her trick of peeling rather than sharpening a pencil, the point held toward her stupendous and sterile bosom swathed in green wool. The way she had of inserting her little finger into her ear and vibrating it very rapidly. The ritual observed every time she gave me a fresh copybook. Always panting a little, her mouth slightly open and emitting in quick succession a series of asthmatic puffs, she would open the copybook to make a margin in it; that is, she would sharply imprint a vertical line with her thumbnail, fold in the edge of the page, press, release, smooth it out with the heel of her hand, after which the book would be briskly twisted around and placed before me ready for use. A new pen followed; she would moisten the glistening nib with susurrous lips before dipping it into the baptismal ink font. Then, delighting in every limb of every limpid letter (especially so because the preceding copybook had ended in utter sloppiness), with exquisite care I would inscribe the word *Dictée* while Mademoiselle hunted through her collection of spelling tests for a good, hard passage.

5

Meanwhile the setting has changed. Hoarfrost and snow have been removed by a silent property man. The summer afternoon is alive with steep clouds breasting the blue. Eyed shadows move on the garden paths. Presently, lessons are over and Mademoiselle is reading to us on the veranda where the mats and plaited chairs develop a spicy, biscuity smell in the heat. On the white windowsills, on the long window seats covered with faded calico, the sun breaks into geometrical gems after passing through rhomboids and squares of stained glass. This is the time when Mademoiselle is at her very best.

What a number of volumes she read through to us on that veranda! Her slender voice sped on and on, never weakening, without the slightest hitch or hesitation, an admirable reading machine wholly independent of her sick bronchial tubes. We got it all: *Les Malheurs de Sophie, Le Tour du Monde en Quatre-Vingts Jours, La Petite Chose, Les Misérables, Le Comte de Monte Cristo,* many others. There she sat, distilling her reading voice from the still prison of her person. Apart from the lips, one of her chins, the smallest but true one, was the only mobile detail of her Buddha-like bulk. The black-rimmed pince-nez reflected eternity. Occasionally a fly would settle on her stern forehead and its three wrinkles would instantly leap up all together like three runners over three hurdles. But nothing whatever changed in the expression of her face—the face I so often tried to depict in my sketchbook, for its impassive and simple symmetry offered a far greater temptation to my stealthy pencil than the bowl of flowers or the decoy duck on the table before me, which I was supposedly drawing.

Presently my attention would wander still farther, and it was then, perhaps, that the rare purity of her rhythmic voice accomplished its true purpose. I looked at a cloud and years later was able to visualize its exact shape. The gardener was pottering among the peonies. A wagtail took a few steps, stopped as if it had remembered something—and then walked on, enacting its name. Coming from nowhere, a comma butterfly settled on the threshold, basked in the sun with its angular fulvous wings spread, suddenly closed them just to show the tiny initial chalked on their underside, and as suddenly darted away. But the most constant source of enchantment during those readings came from the harlequin pattern of colored panes inset in a whitewashed framework on either side of the veranda. The garden when viewed through these magic glasses grew strangely still and aloof. If one looked through blue glass, the sand turned to cinders while inky trees swam in a tropical sky. The yellow created an amber world infused with an extra strong brew of sunshine. The red made the foliage drip ruby dark upon a coral-tinted footpath. The green soaked greenery in a greener green. And when, after such richness, one turned to a small square of normal, savorless glass, with its lone mosquito or lame daddy longlegs, it was like taking a draft of water when one is not thirsty, and one saw a matter-of-fact white bench under familiar trees. But of all the windows this is the pane through which in later years parched nostalgia longed to peer.

Mademoiselle never found out how potent had been the even flow of her voice. The subsequent claims she put forward were quite different. "Ah," she sighed, *"comme on s'aimait!"* ("didn't we love each other!") "Those good old days in the château! The dead wax doll we once buried under the oak!"

(No—a wool-stuffed golliwogg.) "And that time you and Serge ran away and left me stumbling and howling in the depths of the forest!" (Exaggerated.) *"Ah, la fessée que je vous ai flanquée!"* ("My, what a spanking I gave you!") (She did try to slap me once but the attempt was never repeated.) *"Votre tante, la Princesse,* whom you struck with your little fist because she had been rude to me!" (Do not remember.) "And the way you whispered to me your childish troubles!" (Never!) "And the cozy nook in my room where you loved to snuggle because you felt so warm and secure!"

Mademoiselle's room, both in the country and in town, was a weird place to me—a kind of hothouse sheltering a thick-leaved plant imbued with a heavy, queerly acrid odor. Although next to ours, when we were small, it did not seem to belong to our pleasant, well-aired home. In that sickening mist, reeking, among other effluvia, of the brown smell of oxidized apple peel, the lamp burned low, and strange objects glimmered upon the writing desk: a lacquered box with licorice sticks, black segments of which she would hack off with her penknife and put to melt under her tongue; a picture postcard of a lake and a castle with mother-of-pearl spangles for windows; a bumpy ball of tightly rolled bits of silver paper that came from all those chocolates she used to consume at night; photographs of the nephew who had died, of his mother who had signed her picture *Mater Dolorosa,* and of a certain Monsieur de Marante who had been forced by his family to marry a rich widow.

Lording it over the rest was one in a noble frame incrusted with garnets; it showed, in three-quarter view, a slim young brunette clad in a close-fitting dress, with brave eyes and abundant hair. "A braid as thick as my arm and reaching down to my ankles!" was Mademoiselle's melodramatic comment. For this had been she—but in vain did my eyes probe her familiar form to try and extract the graceful creature it had engulfed. Such discoveries as my awed brother and I did make merely increased the difficulties of that task; and the grown-ups who during the day beheld a densely clothed Mademoiselle never saw what we children saw when, roused from her sleep by one of us shrieking himself out of a bad dream, disheveled, candle in hand, a gleam of gilt lace on the blood-red dressing gown that could not quite wrap her quaking mass, the ghastly Jézabel of Racine's absurd play stomped bare-footed into our bedroom.

All my life I have been a poor go-to-sleeper. No matter how great my weariness, the wrench of parting with consciousness is unspeakably repulsive to me. I loathe Somnus, that black-masked headsman binding me to the block; and if in the course of years I have got so used to my nightly ordeal as almost to swagger while the familiar axe is coming out of its great velvet-lined case, initially I had no such comfort or defense: I had nothing—save a door left slightly ajar into Mademoiselle's room. Its vertical line of meek light was something I could cling to, since in absolute darkness my head would swim, just as the soul dissolves in the blackness of sleep.

Saturday night used to be a pleasurable prospect because that was the night Mademoiselle indulged in the luxury of a weekly bath, thus granting a longer lease to my tenuous gleam. But then a subtler torture set in. The nursery bath-room in our St. Petersburg house was at the end of a Z-shaped corridor some twenty heartbeats' distance from my bed, and between dreading Mademoiselle's return from the bathroom to her lighted bedroom and envying my brother's stolid snore, I could never really put my additional time to profit by deftly getting to sleep while a chink in the dark still bespoke a speck of myself in nothingness. At length they would come, those inexorable steps, plodding along the passage and causing some little glass object, which had been secretly sharing my vigil, to tinkle in dismay on its shelf.

Now she has entered her room. A brisk interchange of light values tells me that the candle on her bed table takes over the job of the lamp on her desk. My line of light is still there, but it has grown old and wan, and flickers whenever Mademoiselle makes her bed creak by moving. For I still hear her. Now it is a silvery rustle spelling "Suchard"; now the *trk-trk-trk* of a fruit knife cutting the pages of *La Revue des Deux Mondes*. I hear her panting slightly. And all the time I am in acute distress, desperately trying to coax sleep, opening my eyes every few seconds to check the faded gleam, and imagining paradise as a place where a sleepless neighbor reads an endless book by the light of an eternal candle.

The inevitable happens: the pince-nez case shuts with a snap, the review shuffles onto the marble of the bed table, and gustily Mademoiselle's pursed lips blow; the first attempt fails, a groggy flame squirms and ducks; then comes a second lunge, and light collapses. In that pitchy blackness I lose my bearings, my bed seems to be slowly drifting, panic makes me sit up and stare; finally my dark-adapted eyes sift out, among entoptic floaters, certain more precious blurrings that roam in aimless amnesia until, half-remembering, they settle down as the dim folds of window curtains behind which streetlights are remotely alive.

How utterly foreign to the troubles of the night were those exciting St. Petersburg mornings when the fierce and tender, damp and dazzling arctic spring bundled away broken ice down the sea-bright Neva! It made the roofs shine. It painted the slush in the streets a rich purplish-blue shade which I have never seen anywhere since. Mademoiselle, her coat of imitation seal majestically swelling on her bosom, sat in the back seat of the landau with my brother next to her and me facing them—joined to them by the valley of the lap rug; and as I looked up I could see, strung on ropes from housefront to housefront high above the street, great, tensely smooth, semi-transparent banners billowing, their three wide bands—pale red, pale blue, and merely pale—deprived by the sun and the flying cloud shadows of any too blunt connection with a national holiday, but undoubtedly celebrating now, in the city of memory, the essence of that spring day, the swish of the mud, the ruffled exotic bird with one bloodshot eye on Mademoiselle's hat.

6

She spent seven years with us, lessons getting rarer and rarer and her temper worse and worse. Still, she seemed like a rock of grim permanence when compared to the ebb and flow of English governesses and Russian tutors passing through our large household. She was on bad terms with all of them. Seldom less than a dozen people sat down for meals and when, on birthdays, this number rose to thirty or more, the question of place at table became a particularly burning one for Mademoiselle. Uncles and aunts and cousins would arrive on such days from neighboring estates, and the village doctor would come in his dogcart, and the village schoolmaster would be heard blowing his nose in the cool hall, where he passed from mirror to mirror with a greenish, damp, creaking bouquet of lilies of the valley or a sky-colored, brittle one of cornflowers in his fist.

If Mademoiselle found herself seated too far at the end of the table, and especially if she lost precedence to a certain poor relative who was almost as fat as she (*"Je suis une sylphide à côté d'elle,"* Mademoiselle would say with a shrug of contempt), then her sense of injury caused her lips to twitch in a would-be ironical smile—and when a naïve neighbor would smile back, she would rapidly shake her head, as if coming out of some very deep meditation, with the remark: *"Excusez-moi, je souriais à mes tristes pensées."*

And as though nature had not wished to spare her anything that makes one supersensitive, she was hard of hearing. Sometimes at table we boys would suddenly become aware of two big tears crawling down Mademoiselle's ample cheeks. "Don't mind me," she would say in a small voice, and kept on eating till the unwiped tears blinded her; then, with a heartbroken hiccup she would rise and blunder out of the dining room. Little by little the truth would come out. The general talk had turned, say, on the subject of the warship my uncle commanded, and she had perceived in this a sly dig at her Switzerland that had no navy. Or else it was because she fancied that whenever French was spoken, the game consisted in deliberately preventing her from directing and bejeweling the conversation. Poor lady, she was always in such a nervous hurry to seize control of intelligible table talk before it bolted back into Russian that no wonder she bungled her cue.

"And your Parliament, Sir, how is it getting along?" she would suddenly burst out brightly from her end of the table, challenging my father, who, after a harassing day, was not exactly eager to discuss troubles of the State with a singularly unreal person who neither knew nor cared anything about them. Thinking that someone had referred to music, "But Silence, too, may be beautiful," she would bubble. "Why, one evening, in a desolate valley of the Alps, I actually *heard* Silence." Sallies like these, especially when growing deafness led her to answer questions none had put, resulted in a painful hush, instead of touching off the rockets of a sprightly *causerie*.

And, really, her French was so lovely! Ought one to have

minded the shallowness of her culture, the bitterness of her temper, the banality of her mind, when that pearly language of hers purled and scintillated, as innocent of sense as the alliterative sins of Racine's pious verse? My father's library, not her limited lore, taught me to appreciate authentic poetry; nevertheless, something of her tongue's limpidity and luster has had a singularly bracing effect upon me, like those sparkling salts that are used to purify the blood. This is why it makes me so sad to imagine now the anguish Mademoiselle must have felt at seeing how lost, how little valued was the nightingale voice which came from her elephantine body. She stayed with us long, much too long, obstinately hoping for some miracle that would transform her into a kind of Madame de Rambouillet holding a gilt-and-satin *salon* of poets, princes, and statesmen under her brilliant spell.

She would have gone on hoping had it not been for one Lenski, a young Russian tutor, with mild myopic eyes and strong political opinions, who had been engaged to coach us in various subjects and participate in our sports. He had had several predecessors, none of whom Mademoiselle had liked, but he, as she put it, was *"le comble."* While venerating my father, Lenski could not quite stomach certain aspects of our household, such as footmen and French, which last he considered an aristocratic convention of no use in a liberal's home. On the other hand, Mademoiselle decided that if Lenski answered her point-blank questions only with short grunts (which he tried to Germanize for want of a better language) it was not because he could not understand French, but because he wished to insult her in front of everybody.

I can hear and see Mademoiselle requesting him in dulcet tones, but with an ominous quiver of her upper lip, to pass her the bread; and, likewise, I can hear and see Lenski Frenchlessly and unflinchingly going on with his soup; finally, with a slashing *"Pardon, Monsieur,"* Mademoiselle would swoop right across his plate, snatch up the breadbasket, and recoil again with a *"Merci!"* so charged with irony that Lenski's downy ears would turn the hue of geraniums. "The brute! The cad! The Nihilist!" she would sob later in her room—which was no longer next to ours though still on the same floor.

If Lenski happened to come tripping downstairs while, with an asthmatic pause every ten steps or so, she was working her way up (for the little hydraulic elevator of our house in St. Petersburg would constantly, and rather insultingly, refuse to function), Mademoiselle maintained that he had viciously bumped into her, pushed her, knocked her down, and we already could see him trampling her prostrate body. More and more frequently she would leave the table, and the dessert she would have missed was diplomatically sent up in her wake. From her remote room she would write a sixteen-page letter to my mother, who, upon hurrying upstairs, would find her dramatically packing her trunk. And then, one day, she was allowed to go on with her packing.

7

She returned to Switzerland. World War I came, then the Revolution. In the early twenties, long after our correspondence had fizzled out, by a fluke move of life in exile I chanced to visit Lausanne with a college friend of mine, so I thought I might as well look up Mademoiselle, if she were still alive.

She was. Stouter than ever, quite gray and almost totally deaf, she welcomed me with a tumultuous outburst of affection. Instead of the Château de Chillon picture, there was now one of a garish troika. She spoke as warmly of her life in

Russia as if it were her own lost homeland. Indeed, I found in the neighborhood quite a colony of such old Swiss governesses. Clustering together in a constant seething of competitive reminiscences, they formed a small island in an environment that had grown alien to them. Mademoiselle's bosom friend was now mummylike Mlle. Golay, my mother's former governess, still prim and pessimistic at eighty-five; she had remained in our family long after my mother had married, and her return to Switzerland had preceded only by a couple of years that of Mademoiselle, with whom she had not been on speaking terms when both had been living under our roof. One is always at home in one's past, which partly explains those pathetic ladies' posthumous love for another country, which they never had really known and in which none of them had been very content.

As no conversation was possible because of Mademoiselle's deafness, my friend and I decided to bring her next day the appliance which we gathered she could not afford. She adjusted the clumsy thing improperly at first, but no sooner had she done so than she turned to me with a dazzled look of moist wonder and bliss in her eyes. She swore she could hear every word, every murmur of mine. She could not for, having my doubts, I had not spoken. If I had, I would have told her to thank my friend, who had paid for the instrument. Was it, then, silence she heard, that Alpine Silence she had talked about in the past? In that past, she had been lying to herself; now she was lying to me.

Before leaving for Basle and Berlin, I happened to be walking along the lake in the cold, misty night. At one spot a lone light dimly diluted the darkness. In its nimbus the mist seemed transformed into a visible drizzle. *"Il pleut toujours en Suisse"* was one of those casual comments which, formerly, had made Mademoiselle weep. Below, a wide ripple, almost a wave, and something vaguely white attracted my eye. As I came quite close to the lapping water, I saw what it was—an aged swan, a large, uncouth, dodolike creature, making ridiculous efforts to hoist himself into a moored boat. He could not do it. The heavy, impotent flapping of his wings, their slippery sound against the rocking and plashing boat, the gluey glistening of the dark swell where it caught the light—all seemed for a moment laden with that strange significance which sometimes in dreams is attached to a finger pressed to mute lips and then pointed at something the dreamer has no time to distinguish before waking with a start. But although I soon forgot that dismal night, it was, oddly enough, that night, that compound image—shudder and swan and swell—which first came to my mind when a couple of years later I learned that Mademoiselle had died.

She had spent all her life in feeling miserable; this misery was her native element; its fluctuations, its varying depths, alone gave her the impression of moving and living. What bothers me is that a sense of misery, and nothing else, is not enough to make a permanent soul. My enormous and morose Mademoiselle is all right on earth but impossible in eternity. Have I really salvaged her from fiction? Just before the rhythm I hear falters and fades, I catch myself wondering whether, during the years I knew her, I had not kept utterly missing something in her that was far more she than her chins or her ways or even her French—something perhaps akin to that last glimpse of her, to the radiant deceit she had used in order to have me depart pleased with my own kindness, or to that swan whose agony was so much closer to artistic truth than a drooping dancer's pale arms; something, in short, that I could appreciate only after the things and beings that I had most loved in the security of my childhood had been turned to ashes or shot through the heart.

teenth birthday, and did. Her husband, a great traveler in perfumes, spent most of his time in America, where eventually
he founded a firm and acquired a bit of real estate.

I grew, a happy, healthy child in a bright world of illustrated books, clean sand, orange trees, friendly dogs, sea vis-
tas and smiling faces. Around me the splendid Hotel Mirana
revolved as a kind of private universe, a whitewashed cosmos
within the blue greater one that blazed outside. From the
aproned pot-scrubber to the flanneled potentate, everybody
liked me, everybody petted me. Elderly American ladies leaning on their canes listed toward me like towers of Pisa.
Ruined Russian princesses who could not pay my father
bought me expensive bonbons. He, *mon cher petit papa,* took
me out boating and biking, taught me to swim and dive and
water-ski, read to me *Don Quixote* and *Les Misérables,* and I
adored and respected him and felt glad for him whenever I
overheard the servants discuss his various lady-friends, beautiful and kind beings who made much of me and cooed and
shed precious tears over my cheerful motherlessness.

I attended an English day school a few miles from home,
and there I played rackets and fives, and got excellent marks,
and was on perfect terms with schoolmates and teachers alike.
The only definite sexual events that I can remember as having
occurred before my thirteenth birthday (that is, before I first
saw my little Annabel) were: a solemn, decorous and purely
theoretical talk about pubertal surprises in the rose garden of
the school with an American kid, the son of a then celebrated
motion-picture actress whom he seldom saw in the three-
dimensional world; and some interesting reactions on the part
of my organism to certain photographs, pearl and umbra,
with infinitely soft partings, in Pichon's sumptuous *La Beauté
Humaine* that I had filched from under a mountain of marble-
bound *Graphics* in the hotel library. Later, in his delightful

debonair manner, my father gave me all the information he thought I needed about sex; this was just before sending me, in the autumn of 1923, to a *lycée* in Lyon (where we were to spend three winters); but alas, in the summer of that year, he was touring Italy with Mme de R. and her daughter, and I had nobody to complain to, nobody to consult.

3

Annabel was, like the writer, of mixed parentage: half-English, half-Dutch, in her case. I remember her features far less distinctly today than I did a few years ago, before I knew Lolita. There are two kinds of visual memory: one when you skillfully re-create an image in the laboratory of your mind, with your eyes open (and then I see Annabel in such general terms as: "honey-colored skin," "thin arms," "brown bobbed hair," "long lashes," "big bright mouth"); and the other when you instantly evoke, with shut eyes, on the dark innerside of your eyelids, the objective, absolutely optical replica of a beloved face, a little ghost in natural colors (and this is how I see Lolita).

Let me therefore primly limit myself, in describing Annabel, to saying she was a lovely child a few months my junior. Her parents were old friends of my aunt's, and as stuffy as she. They had rented a villa not far from Hotel Mirana. Bald brown Mr. Leigh and fat, powdered Mrs. Leigh (born Vanessa van Ness). How I loathed them! At first, Annabel and I talked of peripheral affairs. She kept lifting handfuls of fine sand and letting it pour through her fingers. Our brains were turned the way those of intelligent European preadolescents were in our day and set, and I doubt if much individual genius should be assigned to our interest in the plurality of inhabited worlds, competitive tennis, infinity, solipsism and so on. The softness and fragility of baby animals caused us the same intense pain. She wanted to be a nurse in some famished Asiatic country; I wanted to be a famous spy.

All at once we were madly, clumsily, shamelessly, agonizingly in love with each other; hopelessly, I should add, because that frenzy of mutual possession might have been assuaged only by our actually imbibing and assimilating every particle of each other's soul and flesh; but there we were, unable even to mate as slum children would have so easily found an opportunity to do. After one wild attempt we made to meet at night in her garden (of which more later), the only privacy we were allowed was to be out of earshot but not out of sight on the populous part of the *plage.* There, on the soft sand, a few feet away from our elders, we would sprawl all morning, in a petrified paroxysm of desire, and take advantage of every blessed quirk in space and time to touch each other: her hand, half-hidden in the sand, would creep toward me, its slender brown fingers sleepwalking nearer and nearer; then, her opalescent knee would start on a long cautious journey; sometimes a chance rampart built by younger children granted us sufficient concealment to graze each other's salty lips; these incomplete contacts drove our healthy and inexperienced young bodies to such a state of exasperation that not even the cold blue water, under which we still clawed at each other, could bring relief.

Among some treasures I lost during the wanderings of my adult years, there was a snapshot taken by my aunt which showed Annabel, her parents and the staid, elderly, lame gentleman, a Dr. Cooper, who that same summer courted my aunt, grouped around a table in a sidewalk café. Annabel did not come out well, caught as she was in the act of bending over her *chocolat glacé,* and her thin bare shoulders and the parting in her hair were about all that could be identified (as I remember that picture) amid the sunny blur into which her lost loveliness graded; but I, sitting somewhat apart from the rest, came out with a kind of dramatic conspicuousness: a moody, beetle-browed boy in a dark sport shirt and well-tailored white shorts, his legs crossed, sitting in profile, looking away. That photograph was taken on the last day of our fatal summer and just a few minutes before we made our second and final attempt to thwart fate. Under the flimsiest of pretexts (this was our very last chance, and nothing really mattered) we escaped from the café to the beach, and found a desolate stretch of sand, and there, in the violet shadow of some red rocks forming a kind of cave, had a brief session of avid caresses, with somebody's lost pair of sunglasses for only witness. I was on my knees, and on the point of possessing my darling, when two bearded bathers, the old man of the sea and his brother, came out of the sea with exclamations of ribald encouragement, and four months later she died of typhus in Corfu.

4

I leaf again and again through these miserable memories, and keep asking myself, was it then, in the glitter of that remote summer, that the rift in my life began; or was my excessive desire for that child only the first evidence of an inherent singularity? When I try to analyze my own cravings, motives, actions and so forth, I surrender to a sort of retrospective imagination which feeds the analytic faculty with boundless alternatives and which causes each visualized route to fork and re-fork without end in the maddeningly complex prospect of my past. I am convinced, however, that in a certain magic and fateful way Lolita began with Annabel.

I also know that the shock of Annabel's death consolidated the frustration of that nightmare summer, made of it a permanent obstacle to any further romance throughout the cold years of my youth. The spiritual and the physical had been blended in us with a perfection that must remain incomprehensible to the matter-of-fact, crude, standard-brained youngsters of today. Long after her death I felt her thoughts floating through mine. Long before we met we had had the same dreams. We compared notes. We found strange affinities. The same June of the same year (1919) a stray canary had fluttered into her house and mine, in two widely separated countries. Oh, Lolita, had *you* loved me thus!

I have reserved for the conclusion of my "Annabel" phase the account of our unsuccessful first tryst. One night, she managed to deceive the vicious vigilance of her family. In a nervous and slender-leaved mimosa grove at the back of their villa we found a perch on the ruins of a low stone wall. Through the darkness and the tender trees we could see the arabesques of lighted windows which, touched up by the colored inks of sensitive memory, appear to me now like playing cards—presumably because a bridge game was keeping the enemy busy. She trembled and twitched as I kissed the corner of her parted lips and the hot lobe of her ear. A cluster of stars palely glowed above us, between the silhouettes of long thin leaves; that vibrant sky seemed as naked as she was under her light frock. I saw her face in the sky, strangely distinct, as if it emitted a faint radiance of its own. Her legs, her lovely live legs, were not too close together, and when my hand located what it sought, a dreamy and eerie expression, half-pleasure, half-pain, came over those childish features. She sat a little higher than I, and whenever in her solitary ecstasy she was led to kiss me, her head would bend with a sleepy, soft, drooping movement that was almost woeful, and her bare knees caught and compressed my wrist, and slackened again; and her quivering mouth, distorted by the acridity of some mysterious potion, with a sibilant intake of breath came near to my face. She would try to relieve the pain of love by first roughly rubbing her dry lips against mine; then my darling would draw away with a nervous toss of her hair, and then again come darkly near and let me feed on her open mouth, while with a generosity that was ready to offer her everything, my heart, my throat, my entrails, I gave her to hold in her awkward fist the scepter of my passion.

I recall the scent of some kind of toilet powder—I believe she stole it from her mother's Spanish maid—a sweetish, lowly, musky perfume. It mingled with her own biscuity odor, and my senses were suddenly filled to the brim; a sudden commotion in a nearby bush prevented them from overflowing—and as we drew away from each other, and with aching veins attended to what was probably a prowling cat, there came from the house her mother's voice calling her, with a rising frantic note—and Dr. Cooper ponderously limped out into the garden. But that mimosa grove—the haze of stars, the tingle, the flame, the honeydew, and the ache remained with me, and that little girl with her seaside limbs and ardent tongue haunted me ever since—until at last, twenty-four years later, I broke her spell by incarnating her in another.

5

The days of my youth, as I look back on them, seem to fly away from me in a flurry of pale repetitive scraps like those morning snow storms of used tissue paper that a train passenger sees whirling in the wake of the observation car. In my sanitary relations with women I was practical, ironical and brisk. While a college student, in London and Paris, paid ladies sufficed me. My studies were meticulous and intense, although not particularly fruitful. At first, I planned to take a degree in psychiatry as many *manqué* talents do; but I was even more *manqué* than that; a peculiar exhaustion, I am so oppressed, doctor, set in; and I switched to English literature, where so many frustrated poets end as pipe-smoking teachers in tweeds. Paris suited me. I discussed Soviet movies with expatriates. I sat with uranists in the Deux Magots. I published tortuous essays in obscure journals. I composed pastiches:

> . . . Fräulein von Kulp
> may turn, her hand upon the door;
> I will not follow her. Nor Fresca. Nor
> that Gull.

A paper of mine entitled "The Proustian theme in a letter from Keats to Benjamin Bailey" was chuckled over by the six or seven scholars who read it. I launched upon an *"Histoire abrégée de la poésie anglaise"* for a prominent publishing firm, and then started to compile that manual of French literature for English-speaking students (with comparisons drawn from English writers) which was to occupy me throughout the forties—and the last volume of which was almost ready for press by the time of my arrest.

I found a job—teaching English to a group of adults in Auteuil. Then a school for boys employed me for a couple of winters. Now and then I took advantage of the acquaintances I had formed among social workers and psychotherapists to visit in their company various institutions, such as orphanages and reform schools, where pale pubescent girls with matted eyelashes could be stared at in perfect impunity remindful of that granted one in dreams.

Now I wish to introduce the following idea. Between the age limits of nine and fourteen there occur maidens who, to certain bewitched travelers, twice or many times older than they, reveal their true nature which is not human, but nymphic (that is, demoniac); and these chosen creatures I propose to designate as "nymphets."

It will be marked that I substitute time terms for spatial ones. In fact, I would have the reader see "nine" and "fourteen" as the boundaries—the mirrory beaches and rosy rocks—of an enchanted island haunted by those nymphets of mine and surrounded by a vast, misty sea. Between those age limits, are all girl-children nymphets? Of course not. Otherwise, we who are in the know, we lone voyagers, we nympholepts, would have long gone insane. Neither are good looks any criterion; and vulgarity, or at least what a given community terms so, does not necessarily impair certain mysterious characteristics, the fey grace, the elusive, shifty, soul-shattering, insidious charm that separates the nymphet from such coevals of hers as are incomparably more dependent on the spatial world of synchronous phenomena than on that intangible island of entranced time where Lolita plays with her likes. Within the same age limits the number of true nymphets is strikingly inferior to that of provisionally plain, or just nice, or "cute," or even "sweet" and "attractive," ordinary, plumpish, formless, cold-skinned, essentially human little girls, with tummies and pigtails, who may or may not turn into adults of great beauty (look at the ugly dumplings in black stockings and white hats that are metamorphosed into stunning stars of the screen). A normal man given a group photograph of school girls or Girl Scouts and asked to point out the comeliest one will not necessarily choose the nymphet among them.

You have to be an artist and a madman, a creature of infinite melancholy, with a bubble of hot poison in your loins and a super-voluptuous flame permanently aglow in your subtle spine (oh, how you have to cringe and hide!), in order to discern at once, by ineffable signs—the slightly feline outline of a cheekbone, the slenderness of a downy limb, and other indices which despair and shame and tears of tenderness forbid me to tabulate—the little deadly demon among the wholesome children; *she* stands unrecognized by them and unconscious herself of her fantastic power.

Furthermore, since the idea of time plays such a magic part in the matter, the student should not be surprised to learn that there must be a gap of several years, never less than ten I should say, generally thirty or forty, and as many as ninety in a few known cases, between maiden and man to enable the latter to come under a nymphet's spell. It is a question of focal adjustment, of a certain distance that the inner eye thrills to surmount, and a certain contrast that the mind perceives with a gasp of perverse delight. When I was a child and she was a child, my little Annabel was no nymphet to me; I was her equal, a faunlet in my own right, on that same enchanted island of time; but today, in September 1952, after twenty-nine years have elapsed, I think I can distinguish in her the initial fateful elf in my life. We loved each other with a premature love, marked by a fierceness that so often destroys adult lives. I was a strong lad and survived; but the poison was in the wound, and the wound remained ever open, and soon I found myself maturing amid a civilization which allows a man of twenty-five to court a girl of sixteen but not a girl of twelve.

No wonder, then, that my adult life during the European period of my existence proved monstrously twofold. Overtly, I had so-called normal relationships with a number of terrestrial women having pumpkins or pears for breasts; inly, I was consumed by a hell furnace of localized lust for every passing nymphet whom as a law-abiding poltroon I never dared approach. The human females I was allowed to wield were but palliative agents. I am ready to believe that the sensations I derived from natural fornication were much the same as those known to normal big males consorting with their normal big mates in that routine rhythm which shakes the world. The trouble was that those gentlemen had not, and I *had,* caught glimpses of an incomparably more poignant bliss. The dimmest of my pollutive dreams was a thousand times more dazzling than all the adultery the most virile writer of genius or the most talented impotent might imagine. My world was split. I was aware of not one but two sexes, neither of which was mine; both would be termed female by the anatomist. But to me, through the prism of my senses, "they were as different as mist and mast." All this I rationalize now. In my twenties and early thirties, I did not understand my throes quite so clearly. While my body knew what it craved for, my mind rejected my body's every plea. One moment I was ashamed and frightened, another recklessly optimistic. Taboos strangulated me. Psychoanalysts wooed me with pseudoliberations of pseudolibidoes. The fact that to me the only objects of amorous tremor were sisters of Annabel's, her handmaids and girl-pages, appeared to me at times as a forerunner of insanity. At other times I would tell myself that it was all a question of attitude, that there was really nothing wrong in being moved to distraction by girl-children. Let me remind my reader that in England, with the passage of the Children and Young Person Act in 1933, the term "girl-child" is defined as "a girl who is over eight but under fourteen years" (after that, from fourteen to seventeen, the statutory definition is "young person"). In Massachusetts, U.S., on the other hand, a "wayward child" is, technically, one "between seven and seventeen years of age" (who, moreover, habitually associates with vicious or immoral persons). Hugh Broughton, a writer of controversy in the reign of James the First, has proved that Rahab was a harlot at ten years of age. This is all very interesting, and I daresay you see me already frothing at the mouth in a fit; but no, I am not; I am just winking happy thoughts into a little tiddle cup. Here are some more pictures. Here is Virgil who could the nymphet sing in single tone, but probably preferred a lad's perineum. Here are two of King Akhnaten's and Queen Nefertiti's pre-nubile Nile daughters (that royal couple had a litter of six), wearing nothing but many necklaces of bright beads, relaxed on cushions, intact after three thousand years, with their soft brown puppybodies, cropped hair and long ebony eyes. Here are some brides of ten compelled to seat themselves on the fascinum, the virile ivory in the temples of classical scholarship. Marriage and cohabitation before the age of puberty are still not uncommon in certain East Indian provinces. Lepcha old men of eighty copulate with girls of eight, and nobody minds. After all, Dante fell madly in love with his Beatrice when she was nine, a sparkling girleen, painted and lovely, and bejeweled, in a crimson frock, and this was in 1274, in Florence, at a private feast in the merry month of May. And when Petrarch fell madly in love with his Laureen, she was a fair-haired nymphet of twelve running in the wind, in the pollen and dust, a flower in flight, in the beautiful plain as descried from the hills of Vaucluse.

But let us be prim and civilized. Humbert Humbert tried hard to be good. Really and truly, he did. He had the utmost respect for ordinary children, with their purity and vulnerability, and under no circumstances would he have interfered with the innocence of a child, if there was the least risk of a row. But how his heart beat when, among the innocent throng, he espied a demon child, *"enfant charmante et fourbe,"* dim eyes, bright lips, ten years in jail if you only show her you are looking at her. So life went. Humbert was perfectly capable of intercourse with Eve, but it was Lilith he longed for. The bud-stage of breast development appears early (10.7 years) in the sequence of somatic changes accompanying pubescence. And the next maturational item available is the first appearance of pigmented pubic hair (11.2 years). My little cup brims with tiddles.

A shipwreck. An atoll. Alone with a drowned passenger's shivering child. Darling, this is only a game! How marvelous were my fancied adventures as I sat on a hard park bench pretending to be immersed in a trembling book. Around the quiet scholar, nymphets played freely, as if he were a familiar statue or part of an old tree's shadow and sheen. Once a perfect little beauty in a tartan frock, with a clatter put her heavily armed foot near me upon the bench to dip her slim bare arms into me and tighten the strap of her roller skate, and I dissolved in the sun, with my book for fig leaf, as her auburn ringlets fell all over her skinned knee, and the shadow of leaves I shared pulsated and melted on her radiant limb next to my chameleonic cheek. Another time a red-haired school girl hung over me in the *métro*, and a revelation of axillary russet I obtained remained in my blood for weeks. I could list a great number of these one-sided diminutive romances. Some of them ended in a rich flavor of hell. It happened for instance that from my balcony I would notice a lighted window across the street and what looked like a nymphet in the act of undressing before a co-operative mirror. Thus isolated, thus removed, the vision acquired an especially keen charm that made me race with all speed toward my lone gratification. But abruptly, fiendishly, the tender pattern of nudity I had adored would be transformed into the disgusting lamp-lit bare arm of a man in his underclothes reading his paper by the open window in the hot, damp, hopeless summer night.

Rope-skipping, hopscotch. That old woman in black who sat down next to me on my bench, on my rack of joy (a nymphet was groping under me for a lost marble), and asked if I had stomachache, the insolent hag. Ah, leave me alone in my pubescent park, in my mossy garden. Let them play around me forever. Never grow up.

6

A propos: I have often wondered what became of those nymphets later? In this wrought-iron world of criss-cross cause and effect, could it be that the hidden throb I stole from them did not affect *their* future? I had possessed her—and she never knew it. All right. But would it not tell sometime later? Had I not somehow tampered with her fate by involving her image in my voluptas? Oh, it was, and remains, a source of great and terrible wonder.

I learned, however, what they looked like, those lovely, maddening, thin-armed nymphets, when they grew up. I remember walking along an animated street on a gray spring afternoon somewhere near the Madeleine. A short slim girl passed me at a rapid, high-heeled, tripping step, we glanced back at the same moment, she stopped and I accosted her. She came hardly up to my chest hair and had the kind of dimpled round little face French girls so often have, and I liked her long lashes and tight-fitting tailored dress sheathing in pearl-gray her young body which still retained—and that was the nymphic echo, the chill of delight, the leap in my loins—a childish something mingling with the professional *frétillement* of her small agile rump. I asked her price, and she promptly replied with melodious silvery precision (a bird, a very bird!) *"Cent."* I tried to haggle but she saw the awful lone longing in my lowered eyes, directed so far down at her round forehead and rudimentary hat (a band, a posy); and with one beat of her lashes: *"Tant pis,"* she said, and made as if to move away. Perhaps only three years earlier I might have seen her coming home from school! That evocation settled the matter. She led me up the usual steep stairs, with the usual bell clearing the way for the *monsieur* who might not care to meet another *monsieur,* on the mournful climb to the abject room, all bed and *bidet.* As usual, she asked at once for her *petit cadeau,* and as usual I asked her name (Monique) and her age (eighteen). I was pretty well acquainted with the banal way of streetwalkers. They all answer *"dix-huit"*—a trim twitter, a note of finality and wistful deceit which they emit up to ten times per day, the poor little creatures. But in Monique's case there could be no doubt she was, if anything, adding one or two years to her age. This I deduced from many details of her compact, neat, curiously immature body. Having shed her clothes with fascinating rapidity, she stood for a moment partly wrapped in the dingy gauze of the window curtain listening with infantile pleasure, as pat as pat could be, to an organ-grinder in the dust-brimming courtyard below. When I examined her small hands and drew her attention to their grubby fingernails, she said with a naïve frown *"Oui, ce n'est pas bien,"* and went to the washbasin, but I said it did not matter, did not matter at all. With her brown bobbed hair, luminous gray eyes and pale skin, she looked perfectly charming. Her hips were no bigger than those of a squatting lad; in fact, I do not hesitate to say (and indeed this is the reason why I linger gratefully in that gauze-gray room of memory with little Monique) that among the eighty or so *grues* I had had operate upon me, she was the only one that gave me a pang of genuine pleasure. *"Il était malin, celui qui a inventé ce truc-là,"* she commented amiably, and got back into her clothes with the same high-style speed.

I asked for another, more elaborate, assignment later the same evening, and she said she would meet me at the corner café at nine, and swore she had never *posé un lapin* in all her young life. We returned to the same room, and I could not help saying how very pretty she was to which she answered demurely: *"Tu es bien gentil de dire ça"* and then, noticing what I noticed too in the mirror reflecting our small Eden—the dreadful grimace of clenched-teeth tenderness that distorted my mouth—dutiful little Monique (oh, she had been a nymphet all right!) wanted to know if she should remove the layer of red from her lips *avant qu'on se couche* in case I planned to kiss her. Of course, I planned it. I let myself go with her more completely than I had with any young lady before, and my last vision that night of long-lashed Monique is touched up with a gaiety that I find seldom associated with any event in my humiliating, sordid, taciturn love life. She looked tremendously pleased with the bonus of fifty I gave her as she trotted out into the April night drizzle with Humbert Humbert lumbering in her narrow wake. Stopping before a window display she said with great gusto: *"Je vais m'acheter des bas!"* and never may I forget the way her Parisian childish lips exploded on *"bas,"* pronouncing it with an appetite that all but changed the "a" into a brief buoyant bursting "o" as in *"bot."*

I had a date with her next day at 2:15 P.M. in my own rooms, but it was less successful, she seemed to have grown less juvenile, more of a woman overnight. A cold I caught from her led me to cancel a fourth assignment, nor was I sorry to break an emotional series that threatened to burden me with heart-rending fantasies and peter out in dull disappointment. So let her remain, sleek, slender Monique, as she was for a minute or two: a delinquent nymphet shining through the matter-of-fact young whore.

My brief acquaintance with her started a train of thought that may seem pretty obvious to the reader who knows the ropes. An advertisement in a lewd magazine landed me, one brave day, in the office of a Mlle Edith who began by offering me to choose a kindred soul from a collection of rather formal photographs in a rather soiled album *("Regardez-moi cette belle brune!")*. When I pushed the album away and somehow managed to blurt out my criminal craving, she looked as if about to show me the door; however, after asking me what price I was prepared to disburse, she condescended to put me in touch with a person *qui pourrait arranger la chose.* Next day, an asthmatic woman, coarsely painted, garrulous, garlicky, with an almost farcical Provençal accent and a black mustache above a purple lip, took me to what was apparently her own domicile, and there, after explosively kissing the bunched tips of her fat fingers to signify the delectable rosebud quality of her merchandise, she theatrically drew aside a curtain to reveal what I judged was that part of the room where a large and unfastidious family usually slept. It was now empty save for a monstrously plump, sallow, repulsively plain girl of at least fifteen with red-ribboned thick black braids who sat on a chair perfunctorily nursing a bald doll. When I shook my head and tried to shuffle out of the trap, the woman, talking fast, began removing the dingy woolen jersey from the young giantess' torso; then, seeing my determination to leave, she demanded *son argent*. A door at the end of the room was opened, and two men who had been dining in the kitchen joined in the squabble. They were misshapen, bare-necked, very swarthy and one of them wore dark glasses. A small boy and a begrimed, bowlegged toddler lurked behind them.

With the insolent logic of a nightmare, the enraged pro-
curess, indicating the man in glasses, said he had served in the
police, *lui,* so that I had better do as I was told. I went up to
Marie—for that was her stellar name—who by then had quietly transferred her heavy haunches to a stool at the kitchen
table and resumed her interrupted soup while the toddler
picked up the doll. With a surge of pity dramatizing my idiotic gesture, I thrust a banknote into her indifferent hand. She
surrendered my gift to the ex-detective, whereupon I was
suffered to leave.

7

I do not know if the pimp's album may not have been
another link in the daisy-chain; but soon after, for my own
safety, I decided to marry. It occurred to me that regular
hours, home-cooked meals, all the conventions of marriage,
the prophylactic routine of its bedroom activities and, who
knows, the eventual flowering of certain moral values, of
certain spiritual substitutes, might help me, if not to purge
myself of my degrading and dangerous desires, at least to
keep them under pacific control. A little money that had
come my way after my father's death (nothing very grand—
the Mirana had been sold long before), in addition to my
striking if somewhat brutal good looks, allowed me to enter
upon my quest with equanimity. After considerable delibera-
tion, my choice fell on the daughter of a Polish doctor: the
good man happened to be treating me for spells of dizziness
and tachycardia. We played chess: his daughter watched me
from behind her easel, and inserted eyes or knuckles borrowed from me into the cubistic trash that accomplished
misses then painted instead of lilacs and lambs. Let me repeat

with quiet force: I was, and still am, despite *mes malheurs,* an exceptionally handsome male; slow-moving, tall, with soft dark hair and a gloomy but all the more seductive cast of demeanor. Exceptional virility often reflects in the subject's displayable features a sullen and congested something that pertains to what he has to conceal. And this was my case. Well did I know, alas, that I could obtain at the snap of my fingers any adult female I chose; in fact, it had become quite a habit with me of not being too attentive to women lest they come toppling, bloodripe, into my cold lap. Had I been a *français moyen* with a taste for flashy ladies, I might have easily found, among the many crazed beauties that lashed my grim rock, creatures far more fascinating than Valeria. My choice, however, was prompted by considerations whose essence was, as I realized too late, a piteous compromise. All of which goes to show how dreadfully stupid poor Humbert always was in matters of sex.

8

Although I told myself I was looking merely for a soothing presence, a glorified *pot-au-feu,* an animated merkin, what really attracted me to Valeria was the imitation she gave of a little girl. She gave it not because she had divined something about me; it was just her style—and I fell for it. Actually, she was at least in her late twenties (I never established her exact age for even her passport lied) and had mislaid her virginity under circumstances that changed with her reminiscent moods. I, on my part, was as naïve as only a pervert can be. She looked fluffy and frolicsome, dressed *à la gamine,* showed a generous amount of smooth leg, knew how to stress the white of a bare instep by the black of a velvet slipper, and pouted, and dimpled, and romped, and dirndled, and shook her short curly blond hair in the cutest and tritest fashion imaginable.

After a brief ceremony at the *mairie,* I took her to the new apartment I had rented and, somewhat to her surprise, had her wear, before I touched her, a girl's plain nightshirt that I had managed to filch from the linen closet of an orphanage. I derived some fun from that nuptial night and had the idiot in hysterics by sunrise. But reality soon asserted itself. The bleached curl revealed its melanic root; the down turned to prickles on a shaved shin; the mobile moist mouth, no matter how I stuffed it with love, disclosed ignominiously its resemblance to the corresponding part in a treasured portrait of her toadlike dead mama; and presently, instead of a pale little gutter girl, Humbert Humbert had on his hands a large, puffy, short-legged, big-breasted and practically brainless *baba.*

This state of affairs lasted from 1935 to 1939. Her only asset was a muted nature which did help to produce an odd sense of comfort in our small squalid flat: two rooms, a hazy view in one window, a brick wall in the other, a tiny kitchen, a shoe-shaped bath tub, within which I felt like Marat but with no white-necked maiden to stab me. We had quite a few cozy evenings together, she deep in her *Paris-Soir,* I working at a rickety table. We went to movies, bicycle races and boxing matches. I appealed to her stale flesh very seldom, only in cases of great urgency and despair. The grocer opposite had a little daughter whose shadow drove me mad; but with Valeria's help I did find after all some legal outlets to my fantastic predicament. As to cooking, we tacitly dismissed the *pot-au-feu* and had most of our meals at a crowded place in rue Bonaparte where there were wine stains on the table cloth and a good deal of foreign babble. And next door, an art dealer displayed in his cluttered window a splendid, flamboyant, green, red, golden and inky blue, ancient American estampe—a locomotive with a gigantic smokestack, great baroque lamps and a tremendous cowcatcher, hauling its mauve coaches through the stormy prairie night and mixing a lot of spark-studded black smoke with the furry thunder clouds.

These burst. In the summer of 1939 *mon oncle d'Amérique* died bequeathing me an annual income of a few thousand dollars on condition I came to live in the States and showed some interest in his business. This prospect was most welcome to me. I felt my life needed a shake-up. There was another thing, too: moth holes had appeared in the plush of matrimonial comfort. During the last weeks I had kept noticing that my fat Valeria was not her usual self; had acquired a queer restlessness; even showed something like irritation at times, which was quite out of keeping with the stock character she was supposed to impersonate. When I informed her we were shortly to sail for New York, she looked distressed and bewildered. There were some tedious difficulties with her papers. She had a Nansen, or better say Nonsense, passport which for some reason a share in her husband's solid Swiss citizenship could not easily transcend; and I decided it was the necessity of queuing in the *préfecture,* and other formalities, that had made her so listless, despite my patiently describing to her America, the country of rosy children and great trees, where life would be such an improvement on dull dingy Paris.

We were coming out of some office building one morning, with her papers almost in order, when Valeria, as she waddled by my side, began to shake her poodle head vigorously without saying a word. I let her go on for a while and then asked if she thought she had something inside. She answered (I translate from her French which was, I imagine, a translation in its turn of some Slavic platitude): "There is another man in my life."

Now, these are ugly words for a husband to hear. They dazed me, I confess. To beat her up in the street, there and then, as an honest vulgarian might have done, was not feasible. Years of secret sufferings had taught me superhuman self-control. So I ushered her into a taxi which had been invitingly creeping along the curb for some time, and in this comparative privacy I quietly suggested she comment her wild talk. A mounting fury was suffocating me—not because I had any particular fondness for that figure of fun, *Mme Humbert,* but because matters of legal and illegal conjunction were for me alone to decide, and here she was, Valeria, the comedy wife, brazenly preparing to dispose in her own way of my comfort and fate. I demanded her lover's name. I repeated my question; but she kept up a burlesque babble, discoursing on her unhappiness with me and announcing plans for an immediate divorce. *"Mais qui est-ce?"* I shouted at last, striking her on the knee with my fist; and she, without even wincing, stared at me as if the answer were too simple for words, then gave a quick shrug and pointed at the thick neck of the taxi driver. He pulled up at a small café and introduced himself. I do not remember his ridiculous name but after all those years I still see him quite clearly—a stocky White Russian ex-colonel with a bushy mustache and a crew cut; there were thousands of them plying that fool's trade in Paris. We sat down at a table; the Tsarist ordered wine; and Valeria, after applying a wet napkin to her knee, went on talking—*into* me rather than to me; she poured words into this dignified receptacle with a volubility I had never suspected she had in her. And every now and then she would volley a burst of Slavic at her stolid lover. The situation was preposterous and became even more so when the taxi-colonel, stopping Valeria with a possessive smile, began to unfold *his* views and plans. With an atrocious accent to his careful French, he delineated the world of love and

work into which he proposed to enter hand in hand with his
child-wife Valeria. She by now was preening herself, between
him and me, rouging her pursed lips, tripling her chin to pick
at her blouse-bosom and so forth, and he spoke of her as if
she were absent, and also as if she were a kind of little ward
that was in the act of being transferred, for her own good, from
one wise guardian to another even wiser one; and although
my helpless wrath may have exaggerated and disfigured certain impressions, I can swear that he actually consulted me on
such things as her diet, her periods, her wardrobe and the
books she had read or should read. "I think," he said, "she
will like *Jean Christophe*?" Oh, he was quite a scholar, Mr.
Taxovich.

I put an end to this gibberish by suggesting Valeria pack up
her few belongings immediately, upon which the platitudi-
nous colonel gallantly offered to carry them into the car.
Reverting to his professional state, he drove the Humberts to
their residence and all the way Valeria talked, and Humbert
the Terrible deliberated with Humbert the Small whether
Humbert Humbert should kill her or her lover, or both, or
neither. I remember once handling an automatic belonging
to a fellow student, in the days (I have not spoken of them, I
think, but never mind) when I toyed with the idea of enjoying his little sister, a most diaphanous nymphet with a black
hair bow, and then shooting myself. I now wondered if
Valechka (as the colonel called her) was really worth shooting, or strangling, or drowning. She had very vulnerable legs,
and I decided I would limit myself to hurting her very horribly as soon as we were alone.

But we never were. Valechka—by now shedding torrents
of tears tinged with the mess of her rainbow make-up—
started to fill anyhow a trunk, and two suitcases, and a burst-

ing carton, and visions of putting on my mountain boots and taking a running kick at her rump were of course impossible to put into execution with the cursed colonel hovering around all the time. I cannot say he behaved insolently or anything like that; on the contrary, he displayed, as a small sideshow in the theatricals I had been inveigled in, a discreet old-world civility, punctuating his movements with all sorts of mispronounced apologies (*j'ai demannde pardonne*—excuse me—*est-ce que j'ai puis*—may I—and so forth), and turning away tactfully when Valechka took down with a flourish her pink panties from the clothesline above the tub; but he seemed to be all over the place at once, *le gredin,* agreeing his frame with the anatomy of the flat, reading in my chair my newspaper, untying a knotted string, rolling a cigarette, counting the teaspoons, visiting the bathroom, helping his moll to wrap up the electric fan her father had given her, and carrying streetward her luggage. I sat with arms folded, one hip on the window sill, dying of hate and boredom. At last both were out of the quivering apartment—the vibration of the door I had slammed after them still rang in my every nerve, a poor substitute for the backhand slap with which I ought to have hit her across the cheekbone according to the rules of the movies. Clumsily playing my part, I stomped to the bathroom to check if they had taken my English toilet water; they had not; but I noticed with a spasm of fierce disgust that the former Counselor of the Tsar, after thoroughly easing his bladder, had not flushed the toilet. That solemn pool of alien urine with a soggy, tawny cigarette butt disintegrating in it struck me as a crowning insult, and I wildly looked around for a weapon. Actually I daresay it was nothing but middle-class Russian courtesy (with an oriental tang, perhaps) that had prompted the good colonel (Maximovich!

his name suddenly taxies back to me), a very formal person as they all are, to muffle his private need in decorous silence so as not to underscore the small size of his host's domicile with the rush of a gross cascade on top of his own hushed trickle. But this did not enter my mind at the moment, as groaning with rage I ransacked the kitchen for something better than a broom. Then, canceling my search, I dashed out of the house with the heroic decision of attacking him barefisted; despite my natural vigor, I am no pugilist, while the short but broad-shouldered Maximovich seemed made of pig iron. The void of the street, revealing nothing of my wife's departure except a rhinestone button that she had dropped in the mud after preserving it for three unnecessary years in a broken box, may have spared me a bloody nose. But no matter. I had my little revenge in due time. A man from Pasadena told me one day that Mrs. Maximovich née Zborovski had died in childbirth around 1945; the couple had somehow got over to California and had been used there, for an excellent salary, in a year-long experiment conducted by a distinguished American ethnologist. The experiment dealt with human and racial reactions to a diet of bananas and dates in a constant position on all fours. My informant, a doctor, swore he had seen with his own eyes obese Valechka and her colonel, by then gray-haired and also quite corpulent, diligently crawling about the well-swept floors of a brightly lit set of rooms (fruit in one, water in another, mats in a third and so on) in the company of several other hired quadrupeds, selected from indigent and helpless groups. I tried to find the results of these tests in the *Review of Anthropology;* but they appear not to have been published yet. These scientific products take of course some time to fructuate. I hope they will be illustrated with good photographs when they do get printed, although it is not very likely that a prison library will harbor such erudite works. The one to which I am restricted these days, despite my lawyer's favors, is a good example of the inane eclecticism governing the selection of books in prison libraries. They have the Bible, of course, and Dickens (an ancient set, N. Y., G. W. Dillingham, Publisher, MDCCCLXXXVII); and the *Children's Encyclopedia* (with some nice photographs of sunshine-haired Girl Scouts in shorts), and *A Murder Is Announced* by Agatha Christie; but they also have such coruscating trifles as *A Vagabond in Italy* by Percy Elphinstone, author of *Venice Revisited,* Boston, 1868, and a comparatively recent (1946) *Who's Who in the Limelight*—actors, producers, playwrights, and shots of static scenes. In looking through the latter volume, I was treated last night to one of those dazzling coincidences that logicians loathe and poets love. I transcribe most of the page:

Pym, Roland. Born in Lundy, Mass., 1922. Received stage training at Elsinore Playhouse, Derby, N.Y. Made debut in *Sunburst.* Among his many appearances are *Two Blocks from Here, The Girl in Green, Scrambled Husbands, The Strange Mushroom, Touch and Go, John Lovely, I Was Dreaming of You.*

Quilty, Clare, American dramatist. Born in Ocean City, N.J., 1911. Educated at Columbia University. Started on a commercial career but turned to playwriting. Author of *The Little Nymph, The Lady Who Loved Lightning* (in collaboration with Vivian Darkbloom), *Dark Age, The Strange Mushroom, Fatherly Love,* and others. His many plays for children are notable. *Little Nymph* (1940) traveled 14,000 miles and played 280 performances on the road during the winter before ending in New York. Hobbies: fast cars, photography, pets.

Quine, Dolores. Born in 1882, in Dayton, Ohio. Studied

for stage at American Academy. First played in Ottawa in
1900. Made New York debut in 1904 in *Never Talk to Strangers*.
Has disappeared since in [a list of some thirty plays follows].

How the look of my dear love's name even affixed to some
old hag of an actress, still makes me rock with helpless pain!
Perhaps, she might have been an actress too. Born 1935.
Appeared (I notice the slip of my pen in the preceding paragraph, but please do not correct it, Clarence) in *The Murdered
Playwright*. Quine the Swine. Guilty of killing Quilty. Oh,
my Lolita, I have only words to play with!

9

Divorce proceedings delayed my voyage, and the gloom of
yet another World War had settled upon the globe when,
after a winter of ennui and pneumonia in Portugal, I at last
reached the States. In New York I eagerly accepted the soft
job fate offered me: it consisted mainly of thinking up and
editing perfume ads. I welcomed its desultory character and
pseudoliterary aspects, attending to it whenever I had nothing better to do. On the other hand, I was urged by a war-
time university in New York to complete my comparative
history of French literature for English-speaking students.
The first volume took me a couple of years during which I
put in seldom less than fifteen hours of work daily. As I look
back on those days, I see them divided tidily into ample light
and narrow shade: the light pertaining to the solace of
research in palatial libraries, the shade to my excruciating
desires and insomnias of which enough has been said. Knowing me by now, the reader can easily imagine how dusty and
hot I got, trying to catch a glimpse of nymphets (alas, always

remote) playing in Central Park, and how repulsed I was by the glitter of deodorized career girls that a gay dog in one of the offices kept unloading upon me. Let us skip all that. A dreadful breakdown sent me to a sanatorium for more than a year; I went back to my work—only to be hospitalized again.

Robust outdoor life seemed to promise me some relief. One of my favorite doctors, a charming cynical chap with a little brown beard, had a brother, and this brother was about to lead an expedition into arctic Canada. I was attached to it as a "recorder of psychic reactions." With two young botanists and an old carpenter I shared now and then (never very success-fully) the favors of one of our nutritionists, a Dr. Anita John-son—who was soon flown back, I am glad to say. I had little notion of what object the expedition was pursuing. Judging by the number of meteorologists upon it, we may have been tracking to its lair (somewhere on Prince of Wales' Island, I understand) the wandering and wobbly north magnetic pole. One group, jointly with the Canadians, established a weather station on Pierre Point in Melville Sound. Another group, equally misguided, collected plankton. A third studied tuber-culosis in the tundra. Bert, a film photographer—an insecure fellow with whom at one time I was made to partake in a good deal of menial work (he, too, had some psychic troubles)—maintained that the big men on our team, the real leaders we never saw, were mainly engaged in checking the influence of climatic amelioration on the coats of the arctic fox.

We lived in prefabricated timber cabins amid a Pre-Cambrian world of granite. We had heaps of supplies—the *Reader's Digest,* an ice cream mixer, chemical toilets, paper caps for Christmas. My health improved wonderfully in spite or because of all the fantastic blankness and boredom. Sur-rounded by such dejected vegetation as willow scrub and lichens; permeated, and, I suppose, cleansed by a whistling gale; seated on a boulder under a completely translucent sky (through which, however, nothing of importance showed), I felt curiously aloof from my own self. No temptations maddened me. The plump, glossy little Eskimo girls with their fish smell, hideous raven hair and guinea pig faces, evoked even less desire in me than Dr. Johnson had. Nymphets do not occur in polar regions.

I left my betters the task of analyzing glacial drifts, drumlins, and gremlins, and kremlins, and for a time tried to jot down what I fondly thought were "reactions" (I noticed, for instance, that dreams under the midnight sun tended to be highly colored, and this my friend the photographer confirmed). I was also supposed to quiz my various companions on a number of important matters, such as nostalgia, fear of unknown animals, food-fantasies, nocturnal emissions, hobbies, choice of radio programs, changes in outlook and so forth. Everybody got so fed up with this that I soon dropped the project completely, and only toward the end of my twenty months of cold labor (as one of the botanists jocosely put it) concocted a perfectly spurious and very racy report that the reader will find published in the *Annals of Adult Psychophysics* for 1945 or 1946, as well as in the issue of *Arctic Explorations* devoted to that particular expedition; which, in conclusion, was not really concerned with Victoria Island copper or anything like that, as I learned later from my genial doctor; for the nature of its real purpose was what is termed "hush-hush," and so let me add merely that whatever it was, that purpose was admirably achieved.

The reader will regret to learn that soon after my return to civilization I had another bout with insanity (if to melancholia and a sense of insufferable oppression that cruel term must be applied). I owe my complete restoration to a discovery I made while being treated at that particular very expensive sanatorium. I discovered there was an endless source of robust enjoyment in trifling with psychiatrists: cunningly leading them on; never letting them see that you know all the tricks of the trade; inventing for them elaborate dreams, pure classics in style (which make *them,* the dream-extortionists, dream and wake up shrieking); teasing them with fake "primal scenes"; and never allowing them the slightest glimpse of one's real sexual predicament. By bribing a nurse I won access to some files and discovered, with glee, cards calling me "potentially homosexual" and "totally impotent." The sport was so excellent, its results—in *my* case—so ruddy that I stayed on for a whole month after I was quite well (sleeping admirably and eating like a schoolgirl). And then I added another week just for the pleasure of taking on a powerful newcomer, a displaced (and, surely, deranged) celebrity, known for his knack of making patients believe they had witnessed their own conception.

10

Upon signing out, I cast around for some place in the New England countryside or sleepy small town (elms, white church) where I could spend a studious summer subsisting on a compact boxful of notes I had accumulated and bathing in some nearby lake. My work had begun to interest me again— I mean my scholarly exertions; the other thing, my active participation in my uncle's posthumous perfumes, had by then been cut down to a minimum.

One of his former employees, the scion of a distinguished family, suggested I spend a few months in the residence of his impoverished cousins, a Mr. McCoo, retired, and his wife, who wanted to let their upper story where a late aunt had delicately dwelt. He said they had two little daughters, one a baby, the other a girl of twelve, and a beautiful garden, not far from a beautiful lake, and I said it sounded perfectly perfect.

I exchanged letters with these people, satisfying them I was housebroken, and spent a fantastic night on the train, imagining in all possible detail the enigmatic nymphet I would coach in French and fondle in Humbertish. Nobody met me at the toy station where I alighted with my new expensive bag, and nobody answered the telephone; eventually, however, a distraught McCoo in wet clothes turned up at the only hotel of green-and-pink Ramsdale with the news that his house had just burned down—possibly, owing to the synchronous conflagration that had been raging all night in my veins. His family, he said, had fled to a farm he owned, and had taken the car, but a friend of his wife's, a grand person, Mrs. Haze of 342 Lawn Street, offered to accommodate me. A lady who lived opposite Mrs. Haze's had lent McCoo her limousine, a marvelously old-fashioned, square-topped affair, manned by a cheerful Negro. Now, since the only reason for my coming at all had vanished, the aforesaid arrangement seemed preposterous. All right, his house would have to be completely rebuilt, so what? Had he not insured it sufficiently? I was angry, disappointed and bored, but being a polite European, could not refuse to be sent off to Lawn Street in that funeral car, feeling that otherwise McCoo would devise an even more elaborate means of getting rid of me. I saw him scamper away, and my chauffeur shook his head with a soft chuckle. En route, I swore to myself I would not dream of staying in Ramsdale under any circumstance but would fly that very day to the Bermudas or the Bahamas or the Blazes. Possibilities of sweetness or technicolor beaches had been trickling through my spine for some time before, and McCoo's cousin had, in fact, sharply diverted that train of thought with his well-meaning but as it transpired now absolutely inane suggestion.

Speaking of sharp turns: we almost ran over a meddlesome suburban dog (one of those who lie in wait for cars) as we swerved into Lawn Street. A little further, the Haze house, a white-frame horror, appeared, looking dingy and old, more gray than white—the kind of place you know will have a rubber tube affixable to the tub faucet in lieu of shower. I tipped the chauffeur and hoped he would immediately drive away so that I might double back unnoticed to my hotel and bag; but the man merely crossed to the other side of the street where an old lady was calling to him from her porch. What could I do? I pressed the bell button.

A colored maid let me in—and left me standing on the mat while she rushed back to the kitchen where something was burning that ought not to burn.

The front hall was graced with door chimes, a white-eyed wooden thingamabob of commercial Mexican origin, and that banal darling of the arty middle class, van Gogh's "Arlésienne." A door ajar to the right afforded a glimpse of a living room, with some more Mexican trash in a corner cabinet and a striped sofa along the wall. There was a staircase at the end of the hallway, and as I stood mopping my brow (only now did I realize how hot it had been out-of-doors) and staring, to stare at something, at an old gray tennis ball that lay on an oak chest, there came from the upper landing the contralto voice of Mrs. Haze, who leaning over the banisters inquired melodiously, "Is that Monsieur Humbert?" A bit of cigarette ash dropped from there in addition. Presently, the lady herself—sandals, maroon slacks, yellow silk blouse, squarish face, in that order—came down the steps, her index finger still tapping upon her cigarette.

I think I had better describe her right away, to get it over with. The poor lady was in her middle thirties, she had a shiny forehead, plucked eyebrows and quite simple but not unattractive features of a type that may be defined as a weak solution of Marlene Dietrich. Patting her bronze-brown bun, she led me into the parlor and we talked for a minute about the McCoo fire and the privilege of living in Ramsdale. Her very wide-set sea-green eyes had a funny way of traveling all over you, carefully avoiding your own eyes. Her smile was but a quizzical jerk of one eyebrow; and uncoiling herself from the sofa as she talked, she kept making spasmodic dashes at three ashtrays and the near fender (where lay the brown core of an apple); whereupon she would sink back again, one leg folded under her. She was, obviously, one of those women whose polished words may reflect a book club or bridge club, or any other deadly conventionality, but never her soul; women who are completely devoid of humor; women utterly indifferent at heart to the dozen or so possible subjects of a parlor conversation, but very particular about the rules of such conversations, through the sunny cellophane of which not very appetizing frustrations can be readily distinguished. I was perfectly aware that if by any wild chance I became her lodger, she would methodically proceed to do in regard to me what taking a lodger probably meant to her all along, and I would again be enmeshed in one of those tedious affairs I knew so well.

But there was no question of my settling there. I could not be happy in that type of household with bedraggled magazines on every chair and a kind of horrible hybridization between the comedy of so-called "functional modern furniture" and the tragedy of decrepit rockers and rickety lamp tables with dead lamps. I was led upstairs, and to the left— into "my" room. I inspected it through the mist of my utter rejection of it; but I did discern above "my" bed René

Prinet's "Kreutzer Sonata." And she called that servant maid's room a "semi-studio"! Let's get out of here at once, I firmly said to myself as I pretended to deliberate over the absurdly, and ominously, low price that my wistful hostess was asking for board and bed.

Old-world politeness, however, obliged me to go on with the ordeal. We crossed the landing to the right side of the house (where "I and Lo have our rooms"—Lo being presumably the maid), and the lodger-lover could hardly conceal a shudder when he, a very fastidious male, was granted a preview of the only bathroom, a tiny oblong between the landing and "Lo's" room, with limp wet things overhanging the dubious tub (the question mark of a hair inside); and there were the expected coils of the rubber snake, and its complement—a pinkish cozy, coyly covering the toilet lid.

"I see you are not too favorably impressed," said the lady letting her hand rest for a moment upon my sleeve: she combined a cool forwardness—the overflow of what I think is called "poise"—with a shyness and sadness that caused her detached way of selecting her words to seem as unnatural as the intonation of a professor of "speech." "This is not a neat household, I confess," the doomed dear continued, "but I assure you [she looked at my lips], you will be very comfortable, very comfortable, indeed. Let me show you the garden" (the last more brightly, with a kind of winsome toss of the voice).

Reluctantly I followed her downstairs again; then through the kitchen at the end of the hall, on the right side of the house—the side where also the dining room and the parlor were (under "my" room, on the left, there was nothing but a garage). In the kitchen, the Negro maid, a plump youngish woman, said, as she took her large glossy black purse from the knob of the door leading to the back porch: "I'll go now, Mrs. Haze." "Yes, Louise," answered Mrs. Haze with a sigh.

"I'll settle with you Friday." We passed on to a small pantry
and entered the dining room, parallel to the parlor we had
already admired. I noticed a white sock on the floor. With
a deprecatory grunt, Mrs. Haze stooped without stopping
and threw it into a closet next to the pantry. We cursorily
inspected a mahogany table with a fruit vase in the middle,
containing nothing but the still glistening stone of one plum.
I groped for the timetable I had in my pocket and surrepti-
tiously fished it out to look as soon as possible for a train. I
was still walking behind Mrs. Haze through the dining room
when, beyond it, there came a sudden burst of greenery—
"the piazza," sang out my leader, and then, without the least
warning, a blue sea-wave swelled under my heart and, from a
mat in a pool of sun, half-naked, kneeling, turning about on
her knees, there was my Riviera love peering at me over dark
glasses.

It was the same child—the same frail, honey-hued shoulders, the same silky supple bare back, the same chestnut head
of hair. A polka-dotted black kerchief tied around her chest
hid from my aging ape eyes, but not from the gaze of young
memory, the juvenile breasts I had fondled one immortal day.
And, as if I were the fairy-tale nurse of some little princess
(lost, kidnaped, discovered in gypsy rags through which her
nakedness smiled at the king and his hounds), I recognized
the tiny dark-brown mole on her side. With awe and delight
(the king crying for joy, the trumpets blaring, the nurse
drunk) I saw again her lovely indrawn abdomen where my
southbound mouth had briefly paused; and those puerile
hips on which I had kissed the crenulated imprint left by the
band of her shorts—that last mad immortal day behind the
"Roches Roses." The twenty-five years I had lived since then
tapered to a palpitating point, and vanished.

I find it most difficult to express with adequate force that flash, that shiver, that impact of passionate recognition. In the course of the sun-shot moment that my glance slithered over the kneeling child (her eyes blinking over those stern dark spectacles—the little Herr Doktor who was to cure me of all my aches) while I passed by her in my adult disguise (a great big handsome hunk of movieland manhood), the vacuum of my soul managed to suck in every detail of her bright beauty, and these I checked against the features of my dead bride. A little later, of course, she, this *nouvelle,* this Lolita, *my* Lolita, was to eclipse completely her prototype. All I want to stress is that my discovery of her was a fatal consequence of that "princedom by the sea" in my tortured past. Everything between the two events was but a series of gropings and blunders, and false rudiments of joy. Everything they shared made one of them.

I have no illusions, however. My judges will regard all this as a piece of mummery on the part of a madman with a gross liking for the *fruit vert. Au fond, ça m'est bien égal.* All I know is that while the Haze woman and I went down the steps into the breathless garden, my knees were like reflections of knees in rippling water, and my lips were like sand, and—

"That was my Lo," she said, "and these are my lilies."

"Yes," I said, "yes. They are beautiful, beautiful, beautiful!"

A FORGOTTEN POET

1

In 1899, in the ponderous, comfortable padded St. Petersburg of those days, a prominent cultural organization, the
Society for the Advancement of Russian Literature, decided
to honor in a grand way the memory of the poet Konstantin
Perov, who had died half a century before at the ardent age of
four-and-twenty. He had been styled the Russian Rimbaud
and, although the French boy surpassed him in genius, such a
comparison is not wholly unjustified. When only eighteen he
composed his remarkable *Georgian Nights,* a long, rambling
"dream epic," certain passages of which rip the veil of its traditional Oriental setting to produce that heavenly draft which
suddenly locates the sensorial effect of true poetry right
between one's shoulder blades.

This was followed three years later by a volume of poems:
he had got hold of some German philosopher or other, and
several of these pieces are distressing because of the grotesque
attempt at combining an authentic lyrical spasm with a meta-
physical explanation of the universe; but the rest are still as
vivid and unusual as they were in the days when that queer
youth dislocated the Russian vocabulary and twisted the
necks of accepted epithets in order to make poetry splutter

and scream instead of twittering. Most readers like best those
poems of his where the ideas of emancipation, so character-
istic of the Russian fifties, are expressed in a glorious storm of
obscure eloquence, which, as one critic put it, "does not
show you the enemy but makes you fairly burst with the
longing to fight." Personally I prefer the purer and at the same
time bumpier lyrics such as "The Gypsy" or "The Bat."

Perov was the son of a small landowner of whom the only
thing known is that he tried planting tea on his estate near
Luga. Young Konstantin (to use a biographical intonation)
spent most of his time in St. Petersburg vaguely attending
the university, then vaguely looking for a clerical job—little
indeed is known of his activities beyond such trivialities as can
be deduced from the general trends of his set. A passage in the
correspondence of the famous poet Nekrasov, who happened
to meet him once in a bookshop, conveys the image of a
sulky, unbalanced, "clumsy and fierce" young man with "the
eyes of a child and the shoulders of a furniture mover."

He is also mentioned in a police report as "conversing
in low tones with two other students" in a coffeehouse on
Nevsky Avenue. And his sister, who married a merchant from
Riga, is said to have deplored the poet's emotional adventures
with seamstresses and washerwomen. In the autumn of 1849
he visited his father with the special intent of obtaining
money for a trip to Spain. His father, a man of simple reactions, slapped him on the face; and a few days later the poor
boy was drowned while bathing in the neighboring river. His
clothes and a half-eaten apple were found lying under a birch
tree, but the body was never recovered.

His fame was sluggish: a passage from the *Georgian Nights,*
always the same one, in all anthologies; a violent article by the
radical critic Dobrolubov, in 1859, lauding the revolutionary
innuendoes of his weakest poems; a general notion in the

eighties that a reactionary atmosphere had thwarted and finally destroyed a fine if somewhat inarticulate talent—this was about all.

In the nineties, because of a healthier interest in poetry, coinciding as it sometimes does with a sturdy and dull political era, a flurry of rediscovery started around Perov's rhymes while, on the other hand, the liberal-minded were not averse to following Dobrolubov's cue. The subscription for a monument in one of the public parks proved a perfect success. A leading publisher collected all the scraps of information available in regard to Perov's life and issued his complete works in one fairly plump volume. The monthlies contributed several scholarly surveys. The commemorative meeting in one of the best halls of the capital attracted a crowd.

2

A few minutes before the start, while the speakers were still assembled in a committee room behind the stage, the door opened gustily and there entered a sturdy old man, clad in a frock coat that had seen—on his or on somebody else's shoulders—better times. Without paying the slightest heed to the admonishments of a couple of ribbon-badged university students who, in their capacity of attendants, were attempting to restrain him, he proceeded with perfect dignity toward the committee, bowed, and said, "I am Perov."

A friend of mine, almost twice my age and now the only surviving witness of the event, tells me that the chairman (who as a newspaper editor had a great deal of experience in the matter of extravagant intruders) said without even looking up, "Kick him out." Nobody did—perhaps because one is apt to show a certain courtesy to an old gentleman who is

supposedly very drunk. He sat down at the table and, selecting the mildest-looking person, Slavsky, a translator of Long-
fellow, Heine, and Sully-Prudhomme (and later a member of
the terrorist group), asked in a matter-of-fact tone whether
the "monument money" had already been collected, and if
so, when could he have it.

All the accounts agree on the singularly quiet way in which
he made his claim. He did not press his point. He merely
stated it as if absolutely unconscious of any possibility of his
being disbelieved. What impressed one was that at the very
beginning of that weird affair, in that secluded room, among
those distinguished men, there he was with his patriarchal
beard, faded brown eyes, and potato nose, sedately inquiring
about the benefits from the proceedings without even both-
ering to produce such proofs as might have been faked by an
ordinary impostor.

"Are you a relative?" asked someone.

"My name is Konstantin Konstantinovich Perov," said the
old man patiently. "I am given to understand that a descendant of my family is in the hall, but that is neither here nor
there."

"How old are you?" asked Slavsky.

"I am seventy-four," he replied, "and the victim of several
poor crops in succession."

"You are surely aware," remarked the actor Yermakov,
"that the poet whose memory we are celebrating tonight was
drowned in the river Oredezh exactly fifty years ago."

"Vzdor" ("Nonsense"), retorted the old man. "I staged
that business for reasons of my own."

"And now, my dear fellow," said the chairman, "I really
think you must go."

They dismissed him from their consciousness and flocked
out onto the severely lighted platform where another com-

mittee table, draped in solemn red cloth, with the necessary number of chairs behind it, had been hypnotizing the audience for some time with the glint of its traditional decanter. To the left of this, one could admire the oil painting loaned by the Sheremetevski Art Gallery: it represented Perov at twenty-two, a swarthy young man with romantic hair and an open shirt collar. The picture stand was piously camouflaged by means of leaves and flowers. A lectern with another decanter loomed in front and a grand piano was waiting in the wings to be rolled in later for the musical part of the program.

The hall was well packed with literary people, enlightened lawyers, schoolteachers, scholars, eager university students of both sexes, and the like. A few humble agents of the secret police had been delegated to attend the meeting in inconspicuous spots of the hall, as the government knew by experience that the most staid cultural assemblies had a queer knack of slipping into an orgy of revolutionary propaganda. The fact that one of Perov's first poems contained a veiled but benevolent allusion to the insurrection of 1825 suggested taking certain precautions: one never could tell what might happen after a public mouthing of such lines as "the gloomy sough of Siberian larches communicates with the underground ore" *("sibirskikh pikht oogrewmyi shorokh s podzemnoy snositsa roodoy")*.

As one of the accounts has it, "soon one became aware that something vaguely resembling a Dostoyevskian row [the author is thinking of a famous slapstick chapter in *The Possessed*] was creating an atmosphere of awkwardness and suspense." This was due to the fact that the old gentleman deliberately followed the seven members of the jubilee committee onto the platform and then attempted to sit down with them at the table. The chairman, being mainly intent upon avoiding a scuffle in full view of the audience, did his best to make him desist. Under the public disguise of a polite smile he whispered to the patriarch that he would have him ejected from the hall if he did not let go the back of the chair which Slavsky, with a nonchalant air but with a grip of iron, was covertly wresting from under the old man's gnarled hand. The old man refused but lost his hold and was left without a seat. He glanced around, noticed the piano stool in the wings, and coolly pulled it onto the stage just a fraction of a second before the hands of a screened attendant tried to snatch it back. He seated himself at some distance from the table and immediately became exhibit number one.

Here the committee made the fatal mistake of again dismissing his presence from their minds: they were, let it be repeated, particularly anxious to avoid a scene; and moreover, the blue hydrangea next to the picture stand half concealed the obnoxious party from their physical vision. Unfortunately, the old gentleman was most conspicuous to the audience, as he sat there on his unseemly pedestal (with its rotatory potentialities hinted at by a recurrent creaking), opening his spectacle case and breathing fishlike upon his glasses, perfectly calm and comfortable, his venerable head, shabby black clothes, and elastic-sided boots simultaneously suggesting the needy Russian professor and the prosperous Russian undertaker.

The chairman went up to the lectern and launched upon his introductory speech. Whisperings rippled all over the audience, for people were naturally curious to know who the old fellow was. Firmly bespectacled, with his hands on his knees, he peered sideways at the portrait, then turned away from it and inspected the front row. Answering glances could not help shuttling between the shiny dome of his head and the curly head of the portrait, for during the chairman's long speech the details of the intrusion spread, and the imagination of some started to toy with the idea that a poet belonging to an almost legendary period, snugly relegated to it by textbooks, an anachronistic creature, a live fossil in the nets of an ignorant fisherman, a kind of Rip van Winkle, was actually attending in his drab dotage the reunion dedicated to the glory of his youth.

". . . let the name of Perov," said the chairman, ending his speech, "be never forgotten by thinking Russia. Tyutchev has said that Pushkin will always be remembered by our country as a first love. In regard to Perov we may say that he was Russia's first experience in freedom. To a superficial observer this freedom may seem limited to Perov's phenomenal lavishness of poetical images which appeal more to the artist than to the citizen. But we, representatives of a more sober generation, are inclined to decipher for ourselves a deeper, more vital, more human, and more social sense in such lines of his as

When the last snow hides in the shade of the cemetery wall
and the coat of my neighbor's black horse
shows a swift blue sheen in the swift April sun,
and the puddles are as many heavens cupped in the Negro-
hands of the Earth,
then my heart goes out in its tattered cloak
to visit the poor, the blind, the foolish,
the round backs slaving for the round bellies,
all those whose eyes dulled by care or lust do not see
the holes in the snow, the blue horse, the miraculous puddle."

A burst of applause greeted this, but all of a sudden there was a break in the clapping, and then disharmonious gusts of laughter; for, as the chairman, still vibrating with the words he had just uttered, went back to the table, the bearded stranger got up and acknowledged the applause by means of jerky nods and awkward wavings of the hand, his expression combining formal gratitude with a certain impatience. Slavsky and a couple of attendants made a desperate attempt to bundle him away, but from the depth of the audience there arose the cries of "Shame, shame!" and *"Astavte starika!"* ("Leave the old man alone!")

I find in one of the accounts the suggestion that there were accomplices among the audience, but I think that mass compassion, which may come as unexpectedly as mass vindictiveness, is sufficient to explain the turn things were taking. In spite of having to cope with three men the *"starik"* managed to retain a remarkable dignity of demeanor, and when his halfhearted assailants retired and he retrieved the piano stool that had been knocked down during the struggle, there was a murmur of satisfaction. However, the regrettable fact remained that the atmosphere of the meeting was hopelessly impaired. The younger and rowdier members of the audience were beginning to enjoy themselves hugely. The chairman, his nostrils quivering, poured himself out a tumbler of water. Two secret agents were cautiously exchanging glances from two different points of the house.

3

The speech of the chairman was followed by the treasurer's account of the sums received from various institutions and private persons for the erection of a Perov monument in one of the suburban parks. The old man unhurriedly produced a bit of paper and a stubby pencil and, propping the paper on his knee, began to check the figures which were being mentioned. Then the granddaughter of Perov's sister appeared for a moment on the stage. The organizers had had some trouble with this item of the program since the person in question, a fat, popeyed, wax-pale young woman, was being treated for melancholia in a home for mental patients. With twisted mouth and all dressed up in pathetic pink, she was shown to the audience for a moment and then whisked back into the firm hands of a buxom woman delegated by the home.

When Yermakov, who in those days was the darling of theatergoers, a kind of *beau ténor* in terms of the drama, began delivering in his chocolate-cream voice the Prince's speech from the *Georgian Nights,* it became clear that even his best fans were more interested in the reactions of the old man than in the beauty of the delivery. At the lines

> If metal is immortal, then somewhere
> there lies the burnished button that I lost
> upon my seventh birthday in a garden.
> Find me that button and my soul will know
> that every soul is saved and stored and treasured

a chink appeared for the first time in his composure and he slowly unfolded a large handkerchief and lustily blew his nose—a sound which sent Yermakov's heavily adumbrated, diamond-bright eye squinting like that of a timorous steed.

The handkerchief was returned to the folds of the coat and only several seconds *after* this did it become noticeable to the people in the first row that tears were trickling from under his glasses. He did not attempt to wipe them, though once or twice his hand did go up to his spectacles with claw-wise spread fingers, but it dropped again, as if by any such gesture (and this was the culminating point of the whole delicate masterpiece) he was afraid to attract attention to his tears. The tremendous applause that followed the recitation was certainly more a tribute to the old man's performance than to the poem in Yermakov's rendering. Then, as soon as the applause petered out, he stood up and marched toward the edge of the platform.

There was no attempt on the part of the committee to stop him, and this for two reasons. First, the chairman, driven to exasperation by the old man's conspicuous behavior, had gone out for a moment and given a certain order. In the second place, a medley of strange doubts was beginning to unnerve some of the organizers, so that there was a complete hush when the old man placed his elbows on the reading stand.

"And this is fame," he said in such a husky voice that from the back rows there came cries of *"Gromche, gromche!"* ("Louder, louder!")

"I am saying that this is fame," he repeated, grimly peering over his spectacles at the audience. "A score of frivolous poems, words made to joggle and jingle, and a man's name is remembered as if he had been of some use to humanity! No, gentlemen, do not delude yourselves. Our empire and the throne of our father the Tsar still stand as they stood, akin to frozen thunder in their invulnerable might, and the misguided youth who scribbled rebellious verse half a century ago is now a law-abiding old man respected by honest citizens. An old man, let me add, who needs your protection. I am the victim of the elements: the land I had plowed with my sweat, the lambs I had personally suckled, the wheat I had seen waving its golden arms—"

It was then that two enormous policemen quickly and painlessly removed the old man. The audience had a glimpse of his being rushed out—his dickey protruding one way, his beard the other, a cuff dangling from his wrist, but still that gravity and that pride in his eyes.

When reporting the celebration, the leading dailies referred only in passing to the "regrettable incident" that had marred it. But the disreputable *St. Petersburg Record,* a lurid and reactionary rag edited by the brothers Kherstov for the benefit of the lower middle class and of blissfully semiliterate substratum of working people, blazed forth with a series of articles maintaining that the "regrettable incident" was nothing less than the reappearance of the authentic Perov.

4

In the meantime, the old man had been collected by the very wealthy and vulgarly eccentric merchant Gromov, whose household was full of vagabond monks, quack doctors, and "pogromystics." The *Record* printed interviews with the impostor. In these the latter said dreadful things about the "lackeys of the revolutionary party" who had cheated him of his identity and robbed him of his money. This money he proposed to obtain by law from the publishers of Perov's complete works. A drunken scholar attached to the Gromov household pointed out the (unfortunately rather striking) similarity between the old man's features and those of the portrait.

There appeared a detailed but most implausible account of his having staged a suicide in order to lead a Christian life in the bosom of Saint Russia. He had been everything: a peddler, a bird catcher, a ferryman on the Volga, and had wound up by acquiring a bit of land in a remote province. I have seen a copy of a sordid-looking booklet, *The Death and Resurrection of Konstantin Perov,* which used to be sold on the streets by shivering beggars, together with the *Adventures of the Marquis de Sade* and the *Memoirs of an Amazon.*

My best find, however, in looking through old files, is a smudgy photograph of the bearded impostor perched upon the marble of the unfinished Perov monument in a leafless park. He is seen standing very straight with his arms folded;

he wears a round fur cap and a new pair of galoshes but no overcoat; a little crowd of his backers is gathered at his feet, and their little white faces stare into the camera with that special navel-eyed, self-complacent expression peculiar to old pictures of lynching parties.

Given this atmosphere of florid hooliganism and reactionary smugness (so closely linked up with governmental ideas in Russia, no matter whether the Tsar be called Alexander, Nicholas, or Joe), the intelligentsia could hardly bear to visualize the disaster of identifying the pure, ardent, revolutionary-minded Perov as represented by his poems with a vulgar old man wallowing in a painted pigsty. The tragic part was that while neither Gromov nor the Kherstov brothers really believed the purveyor of their fun was the true Perov, many honest, cultivated people had become obsessed by the impossible thought that what they had ejected was Truth and Justice.

As a recently published letter from Slavsky to Korolenko has it: "One shudders to think that a gift of destiny unparalleled in history, the Lazarus-like resurrection of a great poet of the past, may be ungratefully ignored—nay, even more, deemed a fiendish deceit on the part of a man whose only crime has been half a century of silence and a few minutes of wild talk." The wording is muddled but the gist is clear: intellectual Russia was less afraid of falling victim to a hoax than of sponsoring a hideous blunder. But there was something she was still more afraid of, and that was the destruction of an ideal; for your radical is ready to upset everything in the world except any such trivial bauble, no matter how doubtful and dusty, that for some reason radicalism has enshrined.

It is rumored that at a certain secret session of the Society for the Advancement of Russian Literature the numerous insulting epistles that the old man kept sending in were carefully compared by experts with a very old letter written by the poet in his teens. It had been discovered in a certain private archive, was believe to be the only sample of Perov's hand, and none except the scholars who pored over its faded ink knew of its existence. Neither do we know what their findings were.

It is further rumored that a lump of money was amassed and that the old man was approached without the knowledge of his disgraceful companions. Apparently, a substantial monthly pension was to be granted him under the condition that he return at once to his farm and stay there in decorous silence and oblivion. Apparently, too, the offer was accepted, for he vanished as jerkily as he had appeared, while Gromov consoled himself for the loss of his pet by adopting a shady hypnotizer of French extraction who a year or two later was to enjoy some success at the Court.

The monument was duly unveiled and became a great favorite with the local pigeons. The sales of the collected works fizzled out genteelly in the middle of a fourth edition. Finally, a few years later, in the region where Perov had been born, the oldest though not necessarily the brightest inhabitant told a lady journalist that he remembered his father telling him of finding a skeleton in a reedy part of the river.

5

This would have been all had not the Revolution come, turning up slabs of rich earth together with the white rootlets of little plants and fat mauve worms which otherwise would have remained buried. When, in the early twenties, in the dark, hungry, but morbidly active city, various odd cultural institutions sprouted (such as bookshops where famous but destitute writers sold their own books, and so on), somebody or other earned a couple of months' living by arranging a little Perov museum, and this led to yet another resurrection.

The exhibits? All of them except one (the letter). A secondhand past in a shabby hall. The oval-shaped eyes and brown locks of the precious Sheremetevski portrait (with a crack in the region of the open collar suggesting a tentative beheading); a battered volume of the *Georgian Nights* that was thought to have belonged to Nekrasov; an indifferent photograph of the village school built on the spot where the poet's father had owned a house and an orchard. An old glove that some visitor to the museum had forgotten. Several editions of Perov's works distributed in such a way as to occupy the greatest possible space.

And because all these poor relics still refused to form a happy family, several period articles had been added, such as the dressing gown that a famous radical critic had worn in his rococo study, and the chains he had worn in his wooden Siberian prison. But there again, since neither this nor the portraits of various writers of the time were bulky enough, a model of the first railway train to run in Russia (in the forties, between St. Petersburg and Tsarskoye Selo) had been installed in the middle of that dismal room.

The old man, now well over ninety but still articulate in speech and reasonably erect in carriage, would show you around the place as if he were your host instead of being the janitor. One had the odd impression that presently he would lead you into the next (nonexisting) room, where supper would be served. All that he really possessed, however, was a stove behind a screen and the bench on which he slept; but if you bought one of the books exhibited for sale at the entrance he would autograph it for you as a matter of course.

Then one morning he was found dead on his bench by the woman who brought him his food. Three quarrelsome families lived for a while in the museum, and soon nothing remained of its contents. And as if some great hand with a great rasping sound had torn out a great bunch of pages from a number of books, or as if some frivolous story writer had bottled an imp of fiction in the vessel of truth, or as if . . .

But no matter. Somehow or other, in the next twenty years or so, Russia lost all contact with Perov's poetry. Young Soviet citizens know as little about his works as they do about mine. No doubt a time will come when he will be republished and readmired; still, one cannot help feeling that, as things stand, people are missing a great deal. One wonders also what future historians will make of the old man and his extraordinary contention. But that, of course, is a matter of secondary importance.

TIME AND EBB

In the first floriferous days of convalescence after a severe ill-
ness, which nobody, least of all the patient himself, expected
a ninety-year-old organism to survive, I was admonished by
my dear friends Norman and Nura Stone to prolong the lull
in my scientific studies and relax in the midst of some innocent occupation such as brazzle or solitaire.

The first is out of the question, since tracking the name of
an Asiatic town or the title of a Spanish novel through a maze
of jumbled syllables on the last page of the evening news-
book (a feat which my youngest great-granddaughter performs with the utmost zest) strikes me as far more strenuous
than toying with animal tissues. Solitaire, on the other hand,
is worthy of consideration, especially if one is sensitive to its
mental counterpart; for is not the setting down of one's reminiscences a game of the same order, wherein events and
emotions are dealt to oneself in leisurely retrospection?

Arthur Freeman is reported to have said of memoirists that
they are men who have too little imagination to write fiction
and too bad a memory to write the truth. In this twilight of
self-expression I too must float. Like other old men before
me, I have discovered that the near in time is annoyingly con-

fused, whereas at the end of the tunnel there are color and light. I can discern the features of every month in 1944 or 1945, but seasons are utterly blurred when I pick out 1997 or 2012. I cannot remember the name of the eminent scientist who attacked my latest paper, as I have also forgotten those other names which my equally eminent defenders called him. I am unable to tell offhand what year the Embryological Section of the Association of Nature Lovers of Reykjavik elected me a corresponding member, or when, exactly, the American Academy of Science awarded me its choicest prize. (I remember, though, the keen pleasure which both these honors gave me.) Thus a man looking through a tremendous telescope does not see the cirri of an Indian summer above his charmed orchard, but does see, as my regretted colleague, the late Professor Alexander Ivanchenko, twice saw, the swarming of hesperozoa in a humid valley of the planet Venus.

No doubt the "numberless nebulous pictures" bequeathed us by the drab, flat, and strangely melancholic photography of the past century exaggerate the impression of unreality which that century makes upon those who do not remember it; but the fact remains that the beings that peopled the world in the days of my childhood seem to the present generation more remote than the nineteenth century seemed to them. They were still up to their waists in its prudery and prejudice. They clung to tradition as a vine still clings to a dead tree. They had their meals at large tables around which they grouped themselves in a stiff sitting position on hard wooden chairs. Clothes consisted of a number of parts, each of which, moreover, contained the reduced and useless remnants of this or that older fashion (a townsman dressing of a morning had to squeeze something like thirty buttons into as many buttonholes besides tying three knots and checking the contents of fifteen pockets).

In their letters they addressed perfect strangers by what was—insofar as words have sense—the equivalent of "beloved master" and prefaced a theoretically immortal signature with a mumble expressing idiotic devotion to a person whose very existence was to the writer a matter of complete unconcern. They were atavistically prone to endow the community with qualities and rights which they refused to the individual. Economics obsessed them almost as much as theologies had obsessed their ancestors. They were superficial, careless, and shortsighted. More than other generations, they tended to overlook outstanding men, leaving to us the honor of discovering their classics (thus Richard Sinatra remained, while he lived, an anonymous "ranger" dreaming under a Telluride pine or reading his prodigious verse to the squirrels of San Isabel Forest, whereas everybody knew another Sinatra, a minor writer, also of Oriental descent).

Elementary allobiotic phenomena led their so-called spiritualists to the silliest forms of transcendental surmise and made so-called common sense shrug its broad shoulders in equally silly ignorance. Our denominations of time would have seemed to them "telephone" numbers. They played with electricity in various ways without having the slightest notion of what it really was—and no wonder the chance revelation of its true nature came as a most hideous surprise (I was a man by that time and can well remember old Professor Andrews sobbing his heart out on the campus in the midst of a dumbfounded crowd).

But in spite of all the ridiculous customs and complications in which it was entangled, the world of my young days was a gallant and tough little world that countered adversity with a bit of dry humor and would calmly set out for remote battlefields in order to suppress the savage vulgarity of Hitler or Alamillo. And if I let myself go, many would be the bright, and kind, and dreamy, and lovely things which impassioned memory would find in the past—and then woe to the present age, for there is no knowing what a still vigorous old man might do to it if he tucked up his sleeves. But enough of this. History is not my field, so perhaps I had better turn to the personal lest I be told, as Mr. Saskatchewanov is told by the most charming character in present-day fiction (corroborated by my great-granddaughter, who reads more than I do), that "ev'ry cricket ought keep to its picket"—and not intrude on the rightful domain of other "gads and summersmiths."

2

I was born in Paris. My mother died when I was still an infant, so that I can only recall her as a vague patch of delicious lachrymal warmth just beyond the limit of iconographic memory. My father taught music and was a composer himself (I still treasure an ancient program where his name stands next to that of a great Russian); he saw me through my college stage and died of an obscure blood disease at the time of the South American War.

I was in my seventh year when he and I, and the sweetest grandmother a child has ever been blessed with, left Europe, where indescribable tortures were being inflicted by a degenerate nation upon the race to which I belong. A woman in Portugal gave me the hugest orange I had ever seen. From the stern of the liner two small cannon covered its portentously tortuous wake. A party of dolphins performed solemn somersaults. My grandmother read me a tale about a mermaid who had acquired a pair of feet. The inquisitive breeze would join in the reading and roughly finger the pages so as to discover what was going to happen next. That is about all I remember of the voyage.

Upon reaching New York, travelers in space used to be as much impressed as travelers in time would have been by the old-fashioned "skyscrapers"; this was a misnomer, since their association with the sky, especially at the ethereal close of a greenhouse day, far from suggesting any grating contact, was indescribably delicate and serene: to my childish eyes looking across the vast expanse of park land that used to grace the center of the city, they appeared remote and lilac-colored, and strangely aquatic, mingling as they did their first cautious lights with the colors of the sunset and revealing, with a kind of dreamy candor, the pulsating inside of their semitransparent structure.

Negro children sat quietly upon the artificial rocks. The trees had their Latin binomials displayed upon their trunks, just as the drivers of the squat, gaudy, scaraboid motorcabs (generically allied in my mind to certain equally gaudy automatic machines upon the musical constipation of which the insertion of a small coin used to act as a miraculous laxative) had their stale photographic pictures affixed to their backs; for we lived in the era of Identification and Tabulation; saw the personalities of men and things in terms of names and nicknames and did not believe in the existence of anything that was nameless.

In a recent and still popular play dealing with the quaint America of the Flying Forties, a good deal of glamour is infused into the part of the soda jerk, but the side-whiskers and the starched shirtfront are absurdly anachronistic, nor was there in my day such a continuous and violent revolving of tall mushroom seats as is indulged in by the performers. We imbibed our humble mixtures (through straws that were really

much shorter than those employed on the stage) in an atmosphere of gloomy greed. I remember the shallow enchantment
and the minor poetry of the proceedings: the copious froth
engendered above the sunken lump of frozen synthetic cream,
or the liquid brown mud of "fudge" sauce poured over its
polar pate. Brass and glass surfaces, sterile reflections of electric lamps, the whirr and shimmer of a caged propeller, a
Global War poster depicting Uncle Sam and his Rooseveltian
tired blue eyes or else a dapper uniformed girl with a hyper-
trophied nether lip (that pout, that sullen kiss-trap, that transient
fashion in feminine charm—1939–1950), and the unforgettable tonality of mixed traffic noises coming from the street—
these patterns and melodic figures, for the conscious analysis
of which time is alone responsible, somehow connected the
"drugstore" with a world where men tormented metals and
where metals hit back.

I attended a school in New York; then we moved to
Boston; and then we moved again. We seem always to have
been shifting quarters—and some homes were duller than
others; but no matter how small the town, I was sure to find
a place where bicycle tires were repaired, and a place where
ice cream was sold, and a place where cinematographic pictures were shown.

Mountain gorges seemed to have been ransacked for
echoes; these were subjected to a special treatment on a basis
of honey and rubber until their condensed accents could be
synchronized with the labial movements of serial photographs on a moon-white screen in a velvet-dark hall. With a
blow of his fist a man sent a fellow creature crashing into
a tower of crates. An incredibly smooth-skinned girl raised a
linear eyebrow. A door slammed with the kind of ill-fitting
thud that comes to us from the far bank of a river where
woodsmen are at work.

3

I am also old enough to remember the coach trains: as a babe I worshipped them; as a boy I turned away to improved editions of speed. With their haggard windows and dim lights they still lumber sometimes through my dreams. Their hue might have passed for the ripeness of distance, for a blending succession of conquered miles, had it not surrendered its plum-bloom to the action of coal dust so as to match the walls of workshops and slums which preceded a city as inevitably as a rule of grammar and a blot precede the acquisition of conventional knowledge. Dwarf dunce caps were stored at one end of the car and could flabbily cup (with the transmission of a diaphanous chill to the fingers) the grottolike water of an obedient little fountain which reared its head at one's touch.

Old men resembling the hoary ferryman of still more ancient fairy tales chanted out their intermittent "nextations" and checked the tickets of the travelers, among whom there were sure to be, if the journey was reasonably long, a great number of sprawling, dead-tired soldiers and one live, drunken soldier, tremendously peripatetic and with only his pallor to connect him with death. He always occurred singly but he was always there, a freak, a young creature of clay, in the midst of what some very modern history textbooks glibly call Hamilton's period—after the indifferent scholar who put that period into shape for the benefit of the brainless.

Somehow or other my brilliant but unpractical father never could adapt himself to academic conditions sufficiently to stay very long in this or that place. I can visualize all of them, but one college town remains especially vivid: there is no need to name it if I say that three lawns from us, in a leafy lane, stood the house which is now the Mecca of a nation. I remember the sun-splashed garden chairs under the apple tree, and a bright copper-colored setter, and a fat, freckled boy with a book in his lap, and a handy-looking apple that I picked up in the shadow of a hedge.

And I doubt whether the tourists who nowadays visit the birthplace of the greatest man of his time and peer at the period furniture self-consciously huddled beyond the plush ropes of enshrined immortality can feel anything of that proud contact with the past which I owe to a chance incident. For whatever happens, and no matter how many index cards librarians may fill with the titles of my published papers, I shall go down to posterity as the man who had once thrown an apple at Barrett.

To those who have been born since the staggering discoveries of the seventies, and who thus have seen nothing in the nature of flying things save perhaps a kite or a toy balloon (still permitted, I understand, in several states in spite of Dr. de Sutton's recent articles on the subject), it is not easy to imagine airplanes, particularly because old photographic pictures of those splendid machines in full flight lack the life which only art could have been capable of retaining—and oddly enough no greater painter ever chose them as a special subject into which to inject his genius and thus preserve their image from deterioration.

I suppose I am old-fashioned in my attitude toward many aspects of life that happen to be outside my particular branch of science; and possibly the personality of the very old man I am may seem divided, like those little European towns one half of which is in France and the other in Russia. I know this and proceed warily. Far from me is the intention to promote any yearning and morbid regret in regard to flying machines, but at the same time I cannot suppress the romantic undertone which is inherent to the symphonic entirety of the past as I feel it.

In those distant days when no spot on earth was more than sixty hours' flying time from one's local airport, a boy would know planes from propeller spinner to rudder trim tab, and could distinguish the species not only by the shape of the wing tip or the jutting of a cockpit, but even by the pattern of exhaust flames in the darkness; thus vying in the recognition of characters with those mad nature-sleuths—the post-Linnean systematists. A sectional diagram of wing and fuselage construction would give him a stab of creative delight, and the models he wrought of balsa and pine and paper clips provided such increasing excitement during the making that, by comparison, their completion seemed almost insipid, as if the spirit of the thing had flown away at the moment its shape had become fixed.

Attainment and science, retainment and art—the two couples keep to themselves, but when they do meet, nothing else in the world matters. And so I shall tiptoe away, taking leave of my childhood at its most typical point, in its most plastic posture: arrested by a deep drone that vibrates and gathers in volume overhead, stock-still, oblivious of the meek bicycle it straddles, one foot on the pedal, the toe of the other touching the asphalted earth, eyes, chin, and ribs lifted to the naked sky where a warplane comes with unearthly speed which only the expanse of its medium renders unhurried as ventral view changes to rear view, and wings and hum dissolve in the distance. Admirable monsters, great flying machines, they have gone, they have vanished like that flock of swans which passed with a mighty swish of multitudinous wings one spring night above Knights Lake in Maine, from the unknown into the unknown: swans of a species never determined by science, never seen before, never seen since—and then nothing but a lone star remained in the sky, like an asterisk leading to an undiscoverable footnote.

SIGNS AND SYMBOLS

1

For the fourth time in as many years they were confronted with the problem of what birthday present to bring a young man who was incurably deranged in his mind. He had no desires. Man-made objects were to him either hives of evil, vibrant with a malignant activity that he alone could perceive, or gross comforts for which no use could be found in his abstract world. After eliminating a number of articles that might offend him or frighten him (anything in the gadget line for instance was taboo), his parents chose a dainty and innocent trifle: a basket with ten different fruit jellies in ten little jars.

At the time of his birth they had been married already for a long time; a score of years had elapsed, and now they were quite old. Her drab gray hair was done anyhow. She wore cheap black dresses. Unlike other women her age (such as Mrs. Sol, their next-door neighbor, whose face was all pink and mauve with paint and whose hat was a cluster of brookside flowers), she presented a naked white countenance to the fault-finding light of spring days. Her husband, who in the old country had been a fairly successful businessman, was now wholly dependent on his brother Isaac, a real American of almost forty years standing. They seldom saw him and had nicknamed him "the Prince."

That Friday everything went wrong. The underground train lost its life current between two stations, and for a quarter of an hour one could hear nothing but the dutiful beating of one's heart and the rustling of newspapers. The bus they had to take next kept them waiting for ages; and when it did come, it was crammed with garrulous high school children. It was raining hard as they walked up the brown path leading to the sanatorium. There they waited again; and instead of their boy shuffling into the room as he usually did (his poor face botched with acne, ill-shaven, sullen, and confused), a nurse they knew, and did not care for, appeared at last and brightly explained that he had again attempted to take his life. He was all right, she said, but a visit might disturb him. The place was so miserably understaffed, and things got mislaid or mixed up so easily, that they decided not to leave their present in the office but to bring it to him next time they came.

She waited for her husband to open his umbrella and then took his arm. He kept clearing his throat in a special resonant way he had when he was upset. They reached the bus-stop shelter on the other side of the street and he closed his umbrella. A few feet away, under a swaying and dripping tree, a tiny half-dead unfledged bird was helplessly twitching in a puddle.

During the long ride to the subway station, she and her husband did not exchange a word; and every time she glanced at his old hands (swollen veins, brown-spotted skin), clasped and twitching upon the handle of his umbrella, she felt the mounting pressure of tears. As she looked around trying to hook her mind onto something, it gave her a kind of soft shock, a mixture of compassion and wonder, to notice that one of the passengers, a girl with dark hair and grubby red toenails, was weeping on the shoulder of an older woman. Whom did that woman resemble? She resembled Rebecca Borisovna, whose daughter had married one of the Soloveichiks—in Minsk, years ago.

The last time he had tried to do it, his method had been, in the doctor's words, a masterpiece of inventiveness; he would have succeeded, had not an envious fellow patient thought he was learning to fly—and stopped him. What he really wanted to do was to tear a hole in his world and escape.

The system of his delusions had been the subject of an elaborate paper in a scientific monthly, but long before that she and her husband had puzzled it out for themselves. "Referential mania," Herman Brink had called it. In these very rare cases the patient imagines that everything happening around him is a veiled reference to his personality and existence. He excludes real people from the conspiracy—because he considers himself to be so much more intelligent than other men. Phenomenal nature shadows him wherever he goes. Clouds in the staring sky transmit to one another, by means of slow signs, incredibly detailed information regarding him. His inmost thoughts are discussed at nightfall, in manual alphabet, by darkly gesticulating trees. Pebbles or stains or sun flecks form patterns representing in some awful way messages which he must intercept. Everything is a cipher and of everything he is the theme. Some of the spies are detached observers, such as glass surfaces and still pools; others, such as coats in store windows, are prejudiced witnesses, lynchers at heart; others again (running water, storms) are hysterical to the point of insanity, have a distorted opinion of him, and grotesquely misinterpret his actions. He must be always on his guard and devote every minute and module of life to the decoding of the undulation of things. The very air he exhales is indexed and filed away. If only the interest he provokes were limited to his immediate surroundings—but alas it is not! With distance the torrents of wild scandal increase in volume and volubility. The silhouettes of his blood corpuscles, magnified a million times, flit over vast plains; and still farther, great mountains of unbearable solidity and height sum up in terms of granite and groaning firs the ultimate truth of his being.

2

When they emerged from the thunder and foul air of the subway, the last dregs of the day were mixed with the street-lights. She wanted to buy some fish for supper, so she handed him the basket of jelly jars, telling him to go home. He walked up to the third landing and then remembered he had given her his keys earlier in the day.

In silence he sat down on the steps and in silence rose when some ten minutes later she came, heavily trudging upstairs, wanly smiling, shaking her head in deprecation of her silliness. They entered their two-room flat and he at once went to the mirror. Straining the corners of his mouth apart by means of his thumbs, with a horrible masklike grimace, he removed his new hopelessly uncomfortable dental plate and severed the long tusks of saliva connecting him to it. He read his Russian-language newspaper while she laid the table. Still reading, he ate the pale victuals that needed no teeth. She knew his moods and was also silent.

When he had gone to bed, she remained in the living room with her pack of soiled cards and her old albums. Across the narrow yard where the rain tinkled in the dark against some battered ash cans, windows were blandly alight and in one of them a black-trousered man with his bare elbows raised could be seen lying supine on an untidy bed. She pulled the blind down and examined the photographs. As a baby he looked more surprised than most babies. From a fold in the album, a German maid they had had in Leipzig and her fat-faced fiancé fell out. Minsk, the Revolution, Leipzig, Berlin, Leipzig, a slanting housefront badly out of focus. Four years old, in a park: moodily, shyly, with puckered forehead, looking away from an eager squirrel as he would from any other stranger. Aunt Rosa, a fussy, angular, wild-eyed old lady, who had lived in a tremulous world of bad news, bankruptcies, train accidents, cancerous growths—until the Germans put her to death, together with all the people she had worried about. Age six—that was when he drew wonderful birds with human hands and feet, and suffered from insomnia like a grown-up man. His cousin, now a famous chess player. He again, aged about eight, already difficult to understand, afraid of the wallpaper in the passage, afraid of a certain picture in a book which merely showed an idyllic landscape with rocks on a hillside and an old cart wheel hanging from the branch of a leafless tree. Aged ten: the year they left Europe. The shame, the pity, the humiliating difficulties, the ugly, vicious, backward children he was with in that special school. And then came a time in his life, coinciding with a long convalescence after pneumonia, when those little phobias of his which his parents had stubbornly regarded as the eccentricities of a prodigiously gifted child hardened as it were into a dense tangle of logically interacting illusions, making him totally inaccessible to normal minds.

This, and much more, she accepted—for after all living did mean accepting the loss of one joy after another, not even joys in her case—mere possibilities of improvement. She thought of the endless waves of pain that for some reason or other she and her husband had to endure; of the invisible giants hurting her boy in some unimaginable fashion; of the incalculable amount of tenderness contained in the world; of the fate of this tenderness, which is either crushed, or wasted, or transformed into madness; of neglected children humming to themselves in unswept corners; of beautiful weeds that cannot hide from the farmer and helplessly have to watch the shadow of his simian stoop leave mangled flowers in its wake, as the monstrous darkness approaches.

3

It was past midnight when from the living room she heard her husband moan; and presently he staggered in, wearing over his nightgown the old overcoat with astrakhan collar which he much preferred to the nice blue bathrobe he had.

"I can't sleep," he cried.

"Why," she asked, "why can't you sleep? You were so tired."

"I can't sleep because I am dying," he said and lay down on the couch.

"Is it your stomach? Do you want me to call Dr. Solov?"

"No doctors, no doctors," he moaned. "To the devil with doctors! We must get him out of there quick. Otherwise we'll be responsible. Responsible!" he repeated and hurled himself into a sitting position, both feet on the floor, thumping his forehead with his clenched fist.

"All right," she said quietly, "we shall bring him home tomorrow morning."

"I would like some tea," said her husband, and retired to the bathroom.

Bending with difficulty, she retrieved some playing cards and a photograph or two that had slipped from the couch to the floor: knave of hearts, nine of spades, ace of spades, Elsa and her bestial beau.

He returned in high spirits, saying in a loud voice: "I have it all figured out. We will give him the bedroom. Each of us will spend part of the night near him and the other part on this couch. By turns. We will have the doctor see him at least twice a week. It does not matter what the Prince says. He won't have to say much anyway because it will come out cheaper."

The telephone rang. It was an unusual hour for their telephone to ring. His left slipper had come off and he groped for it with his heel and toe as he stood in the middle of the room, and childishly, toothlessly, gaped at his wife. Having more English than he did, it was she who attended to calls.

"Can I speak to Charlie," said a girl's dull little voice.

"What number you want? No. That is not the right number."

The receiver was gently cradled. Her hand went to her old tired heart.

"It frightened me," she said.

He smiled a quick smile and immediately resumed his excited monologue. They would fetch him as soon as it was day. Knives would have to be kept in a locked drawer. Even at his worst he presented no danger to other people.

The telephone rang a second time. The same toneless anxious young voice asked for Charlie.

"You have the incorrect number. I will tell you what you are doing: you are turning the letter O instead of the zero."

They sat down to their unexpected festive midnight tea. The birthday present stood on the table. He sipped noisily; his face was flushed; every now and then he imparted a circular motion to his raised glass so as to make the sugar dissolve more thoroughly. The vein on the side of his bald head where there was a large birthmark stood out conspicuously and, although he had shaved that morning, a silvery bristle showed on his chin. While she poured him another glass of tea, he put on his spectacles and reexamined with pleasure the luminous yellow, green, red little jars. His clumsy moist lips spelled out their eloquent labels: apricot, grape, beech plum, quince. He had got to crab apple, when the telephone rang again.

THE VANE SISTERS

1

I might never have heard of Cynthia's death, had I not run, that night, into D., whom I had also lost track of for the last four years or so; and I might never have run into D. had I not got involved in a series of trivial investigations.

The day, a compunctious Sunday after a week of blizzards, had been part jewel, part mud. In the midst of my usual afternoon stroll through the small hilly town attached to the girls' college where I taught French literature, I had stopped to watch a family of brilliant icicles drip-dripping from the eaves of a frame house. So clear-cut were their pointed shadows on the white boards behind them that I was sure the shadows of the falling drops should be visible too. But they were not. The roof jutted too far out, perhaps, or the angle of vision was faulty, or, again, I did not chance to be watching the right icicle when the right drop fell. There was a rhythm, an alternation in the dripping that I found as teasing as a coin trick. It led me to inspect the corners of several house blocks, and this brought me to Kelly Road, and right to the house where D. used to live when he was instructor here. And as I looked up at the eaves of the adjacent garage with its full display of transparent stalactites backed by their blue silhouettes, I was rewarded at last, upon choosing one, by the sight of what might be described as the dot of an exclamation mark leaving its ordinary position to glide down very fast—a jot faster than the thaw-drop it raced. This twinned twinkle was delightful but not completely satisfying; or rather it only sharpened my appetite for other tidbits of light and shade, and I walked on in a state of raw awareness that seemed to transform the whole of my being into one big eyeball rolling in the world's socket.

Through peacocked lashes I saw the dazzling diamond reflection of the low sun on the round back of a parked automobile. To all kinds of things a vivid pictorial sense had been restored by the sponge of the thaw. Water in overlapping festoons flowed down one sloping street and turned gracefully into another. With ever so slight a note of meretricious appeal, narrow passages between buildings revealed treasures of brick and purple. I remarked for the first time the humble fluting—last echoes of grooves on the shafts of columns—ornamenting a garbage can, and I also saw the rippling upon its lid—circles diverging from a fantastically ancient center. Erect, dark-headed shapes of dead snow (left by the blades of a bulldozer last Friday) were lined up like rudimentary penguins along the curbs, above the brilliant vibration of live gutters.

I walked up, and I walked down, and I walked straight into a delicately dying sky, and finally the sequence of observed and observant things brought me, at my usual eating time, to a street so distant from my usual eating place that I decided to try a restaurant which stood on the fringe of the town. Night had fallen without sound or ceremony when I came out again. The lean ghost, the elongated umbra cast by a parking meter upon some damp snow, had a strange ruddy tinge; this I made out to be due to the tawny red light of the restaurant sign above the sidewalk; and it was then—as I loitered there, wondering rather wearily if in the course of my return tramp I might be lucky enough to find the same in neon blue—it was then that a car crunched to a standstill near me and D. got out of it with an exclamation of feigned pleasure.

He was passing, on his way from Albany to Boston, through the town he had dwelt in before, and more than once in my life have I felt that stab of vicarious emotion followed by a rush of personal irritation against travelers who seem to feel nothing at all upon revisiting spots that ought to harass them at every step with wailing and writhing memories. He ushered me back into the bar that I had just left, and after the usual exchange of buoyant platitudes came the inevitable vacuum which he filled with the random words: "Say, I never thought there was anything wrong with Cynthia Vane's heart. My lawyer tells me she died last week."

2

He was still young, still brash, still shifty, still married to the gentle, exquisitely pretty woman who had never learned or suspected anything about his disastrous affair with Cynthia's hysterical young sister, who in her turn had known nothing of the interview I had had with Cynthia when she suddenly summoned me to Boston to make me swear I would talk to D. and get him "kicked out" if he did not stop seeing Sybil at once—or did not divorce his wife (whom incidentally she visualized through the prism of Sybil's wild talk as a termagant and a fright). I had cornered him immediately. He had said there was nothing to worry about—had made up his mind, anyway, to give up his college job and move with his wife to Albany, where he would work in his father's firm; and the whole matter, which had threatened to become one of those hopelessly entangled situations that drag on for years, with peripheral sets of well-meaning friends endlessly discussing it in universal secrecy—and even founding, among themselves, new intimacies upon its alien woes—came to an abrupt end.

I remember sitting next day at my raised desk in the large classroom where a midyear examination in French Lit. was being held on the eve of Sybil's suicide. She came in on high heels, with a suitcase, dumped it in a corner where several other bags were stacked, with a single shrug slipped her fur coat off her thin shoulders, folded it on her bag, and with two or three other girls stopped before my desk to ask when I would mail them their grades. It would take me a week, beginning from tomorrow, I said, to read the stuff. I also remember wondering whether D. had already informed her of his decision—and I felt acutely unhappy about my dutiful little student as during 150 minutes my gaze kept reverting to her, so childishly slight in close-fitting gray, and kept observing that carefully waved dark hair, that small, small-flowered hat with a little hyaline veil as worn that season, and under it her small face broken into a cubist pattern by scars due to a skin disease, pathetically masked by a sunlamp tan that hardened her features, whose charm was further impaired by her having painted everything that could be painted, so that the pale gums of her teeth between cherry-red chapped lips and the diluted blue ink of her eyes under darkened lids were the only visible openings into her beauty.

Next day, having arranged the ugly copybooks alphabetically, I plunged into their chaos of scripts and came prematurely to Valevsky and Vane, whose books I had somehow misplaced. The first was dressed up for the occasion in a semblance of legibility, but Sybil's work displayed her usual combination of several demon hands. She had begun in very pale, very hard pencil which had conspicuously embossed the black verso, but had produced little of permanent value on the upper side of the page. Happily the tip soon broke, and Sybil continued in another, darker lead, gradually lapsing into the blurred thickness of what looked almost like charcoal, to which, by sucking the blunt point, she had contributed some traces of lipstick. Her work, although even poorer than I had expected, bore all the signs of a kind of desperate conscientiousness, with underscores, transposes, unnecessary footnotes, as if she were intent upon rounding up things in the most respectable manner possible. Then she had borrowed Mary Valevsky's fountain pen and added: *"Cette examain est finie ainsi que ma vie. Adieu, jeunes filles!* Please, *Monsieur le Professeur,* contact *ma soeur* and tell her that Death was not better than D minus, but definitely better than Life minus D."

I lost no time in ringing up Cynthia, who told me it was all over—had been all over since eight in the morning—and asked me to bring her the note, and when I did, beamed through her tears with proud admiration for the whimsical use ("Just like her!") Sybil had made of an examination in French literature. In no time she "fixed" two highballs, while never parting with Sybil's notebook—by now splashed with soda water and tears—and went on studying the death message, whereupon I was impelled to point out to her the grammatical mistakes in it and to explain the way "girl" is translated in American colleges lest students innocently bandy around the French equivalent of "wench," or worse. These rather tasteless trivialities pleased Cynthia hugely as she rose, with gasps, above the heaving surface of her grief. And then, holding that limp notebook as if it were a kind of passport to a casual Elysium (where pencil points do not snap and a dreamy young beauty with an impeccable complexion

winds a lock of her hair on a dreamy forefinger, as she med-
itates over some celestial test), Cynthia led me upstairs to a
chilly little bedroom, just to show me, as if I were the police
or a sympathetic Irish neighbor, two empty pill bottles and
the tumbled bed from which a tender, inessential body, that
D. must have known down to its last velvet detail, had been
already removed.

3

It was four or five months after her sister's death that I began
seeing Cynthia fairly often. By the time I had come to New
York for some vacational research in the Public Library she had
also moved to that city, where for some odd reason (in vague
connection, I presume, with artistic motives) she had taken
what people, immune to gooseflesh, term a "cold water" flat,
down in the scale of the city's transverse streets. What attracted
me was neither her ways, which I thought repulsively viva-
cious, nor her looks, which other men thought striking. She
had wide-spaced eyes very much like her sister's, of a frank,
frightened blue with dark points in a radial arrangement. The
interval between her thick black eyebrows was always shiny,
and shiny too were the fleshy volutes of her nostrils. The
coarse texture of her epiderm looked almost masculine, and,
in the stark lamplight of her studio, you could see the pores of
her thirty-two-year-old face fairly gaping at you like something in an aquarium. She used cosmetics with as much zest as
her little sister had, but with an additional slovenliness that
would result in her big front teeth getting some of the rouge.
She was handsomely dark, wore a not too tasteless mixture of
fairly smart heterogeneous things, and had a so-called good
figure; but all of her was curiously frowzy, after a way I

obscurely associated with left-wing enthusiasms in politics and "advanced" banalities in art, although, actually, she cared for neither. Her coily hairdo, on a part-and-bun basis, might have looked feral and bizarre had it not been thoroughly domesticated by its own soft unkemptness at the vulnerable nape. Her fingernails were gaudily painted, but badly bitten and not clean. Her lovers were a silent young photographer with a sudden laugh and two older men, brothers, who owned a small printing establishment across the street. I wondered at their tastes whenever I glimpsed, with a secret shudder, the higgledy-piggledy striation of black hairs that showed all along her pale shins through the nylon of her stockings with the scientific distinctness of a preparation flattened under glass; or when I felt, at her every movement, the dullish, stalish, not particularly conspicuous but all-pervading and depressing emanation that her seldom bathed flesh spread from under weary perfumes and creams.

Her father had gambled away the greater part of a comfortable fortune, and her mother's first husband had been of Slav origin, but otherwise Cynthia Vane belonged to a good, respectable family. For aught we know, it may have gone back to kings and soothsayers in the mists of ultimate islands. Transferred to a newer world, to a landscape of doomed, splendid deciduous trees, her ancestry presented, in one of its first phases, a white churchful of farmers against a black thunderhead, and then an imposing array of townsmen engaged in mercantile pursuits, as well as a number of learned men, such as Dr. Jonathan Vane, the gaunt bore (1780–1839), who perished in the conflagration of the steamer *Lexington* to become later an habitué of Cynthia's tilting table. I have always wished to stand genealogy on its head, and here I have an opportunity to do so, for it is the last scion, Cynthia, and Cynthia alone, who will remain of any importance in the Vane dynasty.

I am alluding of course to her artistic gift, to her delightful, gay, but not very popular paintings, which the friends of her friends bought at long intervals—and I dearly should like to know where they went after her death, those honest and poetical pictures that illumined her living room—the wonderfully detailed images of metallic things, and my favorite, *Seen Through a Windshield*—a windshield partly covered with rime, with a brilliant trickle (from an imaginary car roof) across its transparent part and, through it all, the sapphire flame of the sky and a green-and-white fir tree.

4

Cynthia had a feeling that her dead sister was not altogether pleased with her—had discovered by now that she and I had conspired to break her romance; and so, in order to disarm her shade, Cynthia reverted to a rather primitive type of sacrificial offering (tinged, however, with something of Sybil's humor), and began to send to D.'s business address, at deliberately unfixed dates, such trifles as snapshots of Sybil's tomb in a poor light; cuttings of her own hair which was indistinguishable from Sybil's; a New England sectional map with an inked-in cross, midway between two chaste towns, to mark the spot where D. and Sybil had stopped on October the twenty-third, in broad daylight, at a lenient motel, in a pink and brown forest; and, twice, a stuffed skunk.

Being as a conversationalist more voluble than explicit, she never could describe in full the theory of intervenient auras that she had somehow evolved. Fundamentally there was nothing particularly new about her private creed since it presupposed a fairly conventional hereafter, a silent solarium of immortal souls (spliced with mortal antecedents) whose main recreation consisted of periodical hoverings over the dear quick. The interesting point was a curious practical twist that Cynthia gave to her tame metaphysics. She was sure that her existence was influenced by all sorts of dead friends each of whom took turns in directing her fate much as if she were a stray kitten which a schoolgirl in passing gathers up, and presses to her cheek, and carefully puts down again, near some suburban hedge—to be stroked presently by another transient hand or carried off to a world of doors by some hospitable lady.

For a few hours, or for several days in a row, and sometimes recurrently, in an irregular series, for months or years, anything that happened to Cynthia, after a given person had died, would be, she said, in the manner and mood of that person. The event might be extraordinary, changing the course of one's life; or it might be a string of minute incidents just sufficiently clear to stand out in relief against one's usual day and then shading off into still vaguer trivia as the aura gradually faded. The influence might be good or bad; the main thing was that its source could be identified. It was like walking through a person's soul, she said. I tried to argue that she might not always be able to determine the exact source since not everybody has a recognizable soul; that there are anonymous letters and Christmas presents which anybody might send; that, in fact, what Cynthia called "a usual day" might be itself a weak solution of mixed auras or simply the routine shift of a humdrum guardian angel. And what about God? Did or did not people who would resent any omnipotent dictator on earth look forward to one in heaven? And wars? What a dreadful idea—dead soldiers still fighting with living ones, or phantom armies trying to get at each other through the lives of crippled old men.

But Cynthia was above generalities as she was beyond

logic. "Ah, that's Paul," she would say when the soup spite-
fully boiled over, or: "I guess good Betty Brown is dead"
when she won a beautiful and very welcome vacuum cleaner
in a charity lottery. And, with Jamesian meanderings that
exasperated my French mind, she would go back to a time
when Betty and Paul had not yet departed, and tell me of
the showers of well-meant, but odd and quite unacceptable,
bounties—beginning with an old purse that contained a
check for three dollars which she picked up in the street and,
of course, returned (to the aforesaid Betty Brown—this is
where she first comes in—a decrepit colored woman hardly
able to walk), and ending with an insulting proposal from an
old beau of hers (this is where Paul comes in) to paint
"straight" pictures of his house and family for a reasonable
remuneration—all of which followed upon the demise of a
certain Mrs. Page, a kindly but petty old party who had
pestered her with bits of matter-of-fact advice since Cynthia
had been a child.

Sybil's personality, she said, had a rainbow edge as if a little
out of focus. She said that had I known Sybil better I would
have at once understood how Sybil-like was the aura of
minor events which, in spells, had suffused her, Cynthia's,
existence after Sybil's suicide. Ever since they had lost their
mother they had intended to give up their Boston home and
move to New York, where Cynthia's paintings, they thought,
would have a chance to be more widely admired; but the old
home had clung to them with all its plush tentacles. Dead
Sybil, however, had proceeded to separate the house from its
view—a thing that affects fatally the sense of home. Right
across the narrow street a building project had come into
loud, ugly, scaffolded life. A pair of familiar poplars died that
spring, turning to blond skeletons. Workmen came and broke

up the warm-colored lovely old sidewalk that had a special violet sheen on wet April days and had echoed so memorably to the morning footsteps of museum-bound Mr. Lever, who upon retiring from business at sixty had devoted a full quarter of a century exclusively to the study of snails.

Speaking of old men, one should add that sometimes these posthumous auspices and interventions were in the nature of parody. Cynthia had been on friendly terms with an eccentric librarian called Porlock who in the last years of his dusty life had been engaged in examining old books for miraculous misprints such as the substitution of *l* for the second *h* in the word "hither." Contrary to Cynthia, he cared nothing for the thrill of obscure predictions; all he sought was the freak itself, the chance that mimics choice, the flaw that looks like a flower; and Cynthia, a much more perverse amateur of mis-shapen or illicitly connected words, puns, logogriphs, and so on, had helped the poor crank to pursue a quest that in the light of the example she cited struck me as statistically insane. Anyway, she said, on the third day after his death she was reading a magazine and had just come across a quotation from an imperishable poem (that she, with other gullible readers, believed to have been really composed in a dream) when it dawned upon her that "Alph" was a prophetic sequence of the initial letters of Anna Livia Plurabelle (another sacred river running through, or rather around, yet another fake dream), while the additional *h* modestly stood, as a private signpost, for the word that had so hypnotized Mr. Porlock. And I wish I could recollect that novel or short story (by some contemporary writer, I believe) in which, unknown to its author, the first letters of the words in its last paragraph formed, as deciphered by Cynthia, a message from his dead mother.

5

I am sorry to say that not content with these ingenious fan-
cies Cynthia showed a ridiculous fondness for spiritualism. I
refused to accompany her to sittings in which paid mediums
took part: I knew too much about that from other sources. I
did consent, however, to attend little farces rigged up by
Cynthia and her two poker-faced gentlemen friends of the
printing shop. They were podgy, polite, and rather eerie old
fellows, but I satisfied myself that they possessed considerable
wit and culture. We sat down at a light little table, and crackling tremors started almost as soon as we laid our fingertips
upon it. I was treated to an assortment of ghosts that rapped
out their reports most readily though refusing to elucidate
anything that I did not quite catch. Oscar Wilde came in and
in rapid garbled French, with the usual anglicisms, obscurely
accused Cynthia's dead parents of what appeared in my jot-
tings as *"plagiatisme."* A brisk spirit contributed the unso-
licited information that he, John Moore, and his brother
Bill had been coal miners in Colorado and had perished in
an avalanche at "Crested Beauty" in January 1883. Frederic
Myers, an old hand at the game, hammered out a piece of
verse (oddly resembling Cynthia's own fugitive productions)
which in part reads in my notes:

> What is this—a conjuror's rabbit,
> Or a flawy but genuine gleam—
> Which can check the perilous habit
> And dispel the dolorous dream?

Finally, with a great crash and all kinds of shudderings and
jiglike movements on the part of the table, Leo Tolstoy visited our little group and, when asked to identify himself by

specific traits of terrene habitation, launched upon a complex description of what seemed to be some Russian type of architectural woodwork ("figures on boards—man, horse, cock, man, horse, cock"), all of which was difficult to take down, hard to understand, and impossible to verify.

I attended two or three other sittings which were even sillier but I must confess that I preferred the childish entertainment they afforded and the cider we drank (Podgy and Pudgy were teetotalers) to Cynthia's awful house parties.

She gave them at the Wheelers' nice flat next door—the sort of arrangement dear to her centrifugal nature, but then, of course, her own living room always looked like a dirty old palette. Following a barbaric, unhygienic, and adulterous custom, the guests' coats, still warm on the inside, were carried by quiet, baldish Bob Wheeler into the sanctity of a tidy bedroom and heaped on the conjugal bed. It was also he who poured out the drinks, which were passed around by the young photographer while Cynthia and Mrs. Wheeler took care of the canapés.

A late arrival had the impression of lots of loud people unnecessarily grouped within a smoke-blue space between two mirrors gorged with reflections. Because, I suppose, Cynthia wished to be the youngest in the room, the women she used to invite, married or single, were, at the best, in their precarious forties; some of them would bring from their homes, in dark taxis, intact vestiges of good looks, which, however, they lost as the party progressed. It has always amazed me the ability sociable weekend revelers have of finding almost at once, by a purely empiric but very precise method, a common denominator of drunkenness, to which everybody loyally sticks before descending, all together, to the next level. The rich friendliness of the matrons was marked by tomboyish overtones, while the fixed inward look of amiably tight men was like a sacrilegious parody of pregnancy. Although some of the guests were connected in one way or another with the arts, there was no inspired talk, no wreathed, elbow-propped heads, and of course no flute girls. From some vantage point where she had been sitting in a stranded mermaid pose on the pale carpet with one or two younger fellows, Cynthia, her face varnished with a film of beaming sweat, would creep up on her knees, a proffered plate of nuts in one hand, and crisply tap with the other the athletic leg of Cochran or Corcoran, an art dealer, ensconced, on a pearl-gray sofa, between two flushed, happily disintegrating ladies.

At a further stage there would come spurts of more riotous gaiety. Corcoran or Coransky would grab Cynthia or some other wandering woman by the shoulder and lead her into a corner to confront her with a grinning imbroglio of private jokes and rumors, whereupon, with a laugh and a toss of her head, she would break away. And still later there would be flurries of intersexual chumminess, jocular reconciliations, a bare fleshy arm flung around another woman's husband (he standing very upright in the midst of a swaying room), or a sudden rush of flirtatious anger, of clumsy pursuit—and the quiet half-smile of Bob Wheeler picking up glasses that grew like mushrooms in the shade of chairs.

After one last party of that sort, I wrote Cynthia a perfectly harmless and, on the whole, well-meant note, in which I poked a little Latin fun at some of her guests. I also apologized for not having touched her whiskey, saying that as a Frenchman I preferred the grape to the grain. A few days later I met her on the steps of the Public Library, in the broken sun, under a weak cloudburst, opening her amber umbrella, struggling with a couple of armpitted books (of which I relieved her for a moment), *Footfalls on the Boundary of Another World* by Robert Dale Owen, and something on "Spiritual-

ism and Christianity"; when, suddenly, with no provocation
on my part, she blazed out at me with vulgar vehemence,
using poisonous words, saying—through pear-shaped drops
of sparse rain—that I was a prig and a snob; that I only saw
the gestures and disguises of people; that Corcoran had res-
cued from drowning, in two different oceans, two men—by
an irrelevant coincidence both called Corcoran; that romping
and screeching Joan Winter had a little girl doomed to grow
completely blind in a few months; and that the woman in
green with the freckled chest whom I had snubbed in some
way or other had written a national best-seller in 1932.
Strange Cynthia! I had been told she could be thunderously
rude to people whom she liked and respected; one had, however, to draw the line somewhere and since I had by then sufficiently studied her interesting auras and other odds and ids,
I decided to stop seeing her altogether.

6

The night D. informed me of Cynthia's death I returned after
eleven to the two-story house I shared, in horizontal section,
with an emeritus professor's widow. Upon reaching the porch
I looked with the apprehension of solitude at the two kinds
of darkness in the two rows of windows: the darkness of
absence and the darkness of sleep.

I could do something about the first but could not dupli-
cate the second. My bed gave me no sense of safety; its
springs only made my nerves bounce. I plunged into Shake-
speare's sonnets—and found myself idiotically checking the
first letters of the lines to see what sacramental words they
might form. I got FATE (LXX), ATOM (CXX), and, twice,
TAFT (LXXXVIII, CXXXI). Every now and then I would

glance around to see how the objects in my room were behaving. It was strange to think that if bombs began to fall I would feel little more than a gambler's excitement (and a great deal of earthy relief) whereas my heart would burst if a certain suspiciously tense-looking little bottle on yonder shelf moved a fraction of an inch to one side. The silence, too, was suspiciously compact as if deliberately forming a black backdrop for the nerve flash caused by any small sound of unknown origin. All traffic was dead. In vain did I pray for the groan of a truck up Perkins Street. The woman above who used to drive me crazy by the booming thuds occasioned by what seemed monstrous feet of stone (actually, in diurnal life, she was a small dumpy creature resembling a mummified guinea pig) would have earned my blessings had she now trudged to her bathroom. I put out my light and cleared my throat several times so as to be responsible for at least *that* sound. I thumbed a mental ride with a very remote automobile but it dropped me before I had a chance to doze off. Presently a crackle (due, I hoped, to a discarded and crushed sheet of paper opening like a mean, stubborn night flower) started and stopped in the wastepaper basket, and my bed table responded with a little click. It would have been just like Cynthia to put on right then a cheap poltergeist show.

I decided to fight Cynthia. I reviewed in thought the modern era of raps and apparitions, beginning with the knockings of 1848, at the hamlet of Hydesville, New York, and ending with grotesque phenomena at Cambridge, Massachusetts; I evoked the ankle bones and other anatomical castanets of the Fox sisters (as described by the sages of the University of Buffalo); the mysteriously uniform type of delicate adolescent in bleak Epworth or Tedworth, radiating the same disturbances as in old Peru; solemn Victorian orgies with roses falling and accordions floating to the strains of sacred music; professional imposters regurgitating moist cheesecloth; Mr. Duncan, a lady medium's dignified husband, who, when asked if he would submit to a search, excused himself on the ground of soiled underwear; old Alfred Russel Wallace, the naïve naturalist, refusing to believe that the white form with bare feet and unperforated earlobes before him, at a private pandemonium in Boston, could be prim Miss Cook whom he had just seen asleep, in her curtained corner, all dressed in black, wearing laced-up boots and earrings; two other investigators, small, puny, but reasonably intelligent and active men, closely clinging with arms and legs about Eusapia, a large, plump elderly female reeking of garlic, who still managed to fool them; and the skeptical and embarrassed magician, instructed by charming young Margery's "control" not to get lost in the bathrobe's lining but to follow up the left stocking until he reached the bare thigh—upon the warm skin of which he felt a "teleplastic" mass that appeared to the touch uncommonly like cold, uncooked liver.

7

I was appealing to flesh, and the corruption of flesh, to refute and defeat the possible persistence of discarnate life. Alas, these conjurations only enhanced my fear of Cynthia's phantom. Atavistic peace came with dawn, and when I slipped into sleep the sun through the tawny window shades penetrated a dream that somehow was full of Cynthia.

This was disappointing. Secure in the fortress of daylight, I said to myself that I had expected more. She, a painter of glass-bright minutiae—and now so vague! I lay in bed, thinking my dream over and listening to the sparrows outside: Who knows, if recorded and then run backward, those bird sounds might not become human speech, voiced words, just as the latter become a twitter when reversed? I set myself to reread my dream—backward, diagonally, up, down—trying hard to unravel something Cynthia-like in it, something strange and suggestive that must be there.

I could isolate, consciously, little. Everything seemed blurred, yellow-clouded, yielding nothing tangible. Her inept acrostics, maudlin evasions, theopathies—every recollection formed ripples of mysterious meaning. Everything seemed yellowly blurred, illusive, lost.

LANCE

The name of the planet, presuming it has already received one, is immaterial. At its most favorable opposition, it may very well be separated from the earth by only as many miles as there are years between last Friday and the rise of the Himalayas—a million times the reader's average age. In the telescopic field of one's fancy, through the prism of one's tears, any particularities it presents should be no more striking than those of existing planets. A rosy globe, marbled with dusky blotches, it is one of the countless objects diligently revolving in the infinite and gratuitous awfulness of fluid space.

My planet's *maria* (which are not seas) and its *lacus* (which are not lakes) have also, let us suppose, received names; some less jejune, perhaps, than those of garden roses; others, more pointless than the surnames of their observers (for, to take actual cases, that an astronomer should have been called Lampland is as marvelous as that an entomologist should have been called Krautwurm); but most of them of so antique a style as to vie in sonorous and corrupt enchantment with place names pertaining to romances of chivalry.

Just as our Pinedales, down here, have often little to offer beyond a shoe factory on one side of the tracks and the rusty inferno of an automobile dump on the other, so those seductive Arcadias and Icarias and Zephyrias on planetary maps may quite likely turn out to be dead deserts lacking even the milkweed that graces our dumps. Selenographers will confirm this, but then, their lenses serve them better than ours do. In the present instance, the greater the magnification, the more the mottling of the planet's surface looks as if it were seen by a submerged swimmer peering up through semitranslucent water. And if certain connected markings resemble in a shadowy way the line-and-hole pattern of a Chinese-checkers board, let us consider them geometrical hallucinations.

I not only debar a too definite planet from any role in my story—from the role every dot and full stop should play in my story (which I see as a kind of celestial chart)—I also refuse to have anything to do with those technical prophecies that scientists are reported to make to reporters. Not for me is the rocket racket. Not for me are the artificial little satellites that the earth is promised; landing starstrips for spaceships ("spacers")—one, two, three, four, and then thousands of strong castles in the air each complete with cookhouse and keep, set up by terrestrial nations in a frenzy of competitive confusion, phony gravitation, and savagely flapping flags.

Another thing I have not the slightest use for is the special-equipment business—the airtight suit, the oxygen apparatus—suchlike contraptions. Like old Mr. Boke, of whom we shall hear in a minute, I am eminently qualified to dismiss these practical matters (which anyway are doomed to seem absurdly impractical to future spaceshipmen, such as old Boke's only son), since the emotions that gadgets provoke in me range from dull distrust to morbid trepidation. Only by a heroic effort can I make myself unscrew a bulb that has died an inexplicable death and screw in another, which will light up in my face with the hideous instancy of a dragon's egg hatching in one's bare hand.

Finally, I utterly spurn and reject so-called science fiction. I have looked into it, and found it as boring as the mystery-story magazines—the same sort of dismally pedestrian writing with oodles of dialogue and loads of commutational humor. The clichés are, of course, disguised; essentially, they are the same throughout all cheap reading matter, whether it spans the universe or the living room. They are like those "assorted" cookies that differ from one another only in shape and shade, whereby their shrewd makers ensnare the salivating consumer in a mad Pavlovian world where, at no extra cost, variations in simple visual values influence and gradually replace flavor, which thus goes the way of talent and truth.

So the good guy grins, and the villain sneers, and a noble heart sports a slangy speech. Star tsars, directors of Galactic Unions, are practically replicas of those peppy, red-haired executives in earthy earth jobs, that illustrate with their little crinkles the human interest stories of the well-thumbed slicks in beauty parlors. Invaders of Denebola and Spica, Virgo's finest, bear names beginning with Mac; cold scientists are usually found under Steins; some of them share with the super-galactic gals such abstract labels as Biola or Vala. Inhabitants of foreign planets, "intelligent" beings, humanoid or of various mythic makes, have one remarkable trait in common: their intimate structure is never depicted. In a supreme concession to biped propriety, not only do centaurs wear loincloths; they wear them about their forelegs.

This seems to complete the elimination—unless anybody wants to discuss the question of time? Here again, in order to focalize young Emery L. Boke, that more or less remote descendant of mine who is to be a member of the first interplanetary expedition (which, after all, is the one humble pos-

tulate of my tale), I gladly leave the replacement by a preten-
tious "2" or "3" of the honest "1" in our "1900" to the capable paws of *Starzan* and other comics and atomics. Let it be
2145 A.D. or 200 A.A., it does not matter. I have no desire to
barge into vested interests of any kind. This is strictly an amateur performance, with quite casual stage properties and a minimum of scenery, and the quilled remains of a dead porcupine
in a corner of the old barn. We are here among friends, the
Browns and the Bensons, the Whites and the Wilsons, and
when somebody goes out for a smoke, he hears the crickets,
and a distant farm dog (who waits, between barks, to listen to
what we cannot hear). The summer night sky is a mess of stars.
Emery Lancelot Boke, at twenty-one, knows immeasurably
more about them than I, who am fifty and terrified.

2

Lance is tall and lean, with thick tendons and greenish veins
on his suntanned forearms and a scar on his brow. When doing
nothing—when sitting all at ease as he sits now, leaning forward from the edge of a low armchair, his shoulders hunched
up, his elbows propped on his big knees—he has a way of
slowly clasping and unclasping his handsome hands, a gesture
I borrow for him from one of his ancestors. An air of gravity,
of uncomfortable concentration (all thought is uncomfortable, and young thought especially so), is his usual expression;
at the moment, however, it is a manner of mask, concealing
his furious desire to get rid of a long-drawn tension. As a rule,
he does not smile often, and besides, "smile" is too smooth a
word for the abrupt, bright contortion that now suddenly
illumes his mouth and eyes as the shoulders hunch higher, the
moving hands stop in a clasped position, and he lightly stamps

the toe of one foot. His parents are in the room, and also a chance visitor, a fool and a bore, who is not aware of what is happening—for this is an awkward moment in a gloomy house on the eve of a fabulous departure.

An hour goes by. At last the visitor picks up his top hat from the carpet and leaves. Lance remains alone with his parents, which only serves to increase the tension. Mr. Boke I see plainly enough. But I cannot visualize Mrs. Boke with any degree of clarity, no matter how deep I sink into my difficult trance. I know that her cheerfulness—small talk, quick beat of eyelashes—is something she keeps up not so much for the sake of her son as for that of her husband, and his aging heart, and old Boke realizes this only too well and, on top of his own monstrous anguish, he has to cope with her feigned levity, which disturbs him more than would an utter and unconditional collapse. I am somewhat disappointed that I cannot make out her features. All I manage to glimpse is an effect of melting light on one side of her misty hair, and in this, I suspect, I am insidiously influenced by the standard artistry of modern photography and I feel how much easier writing must have been in former days when one's imagination was not hemmed in by innumerable visual aids, and a frontiersman looking at his first giant cactus or his first high snows was not necessarily reminded of a tire company's pictorial advertisement.

In the case of Mr. Boke, I find myself operating with the features of an old professor of history, a brilliant medievalist, whose white whiskers, pink pate, and black suit are famous on a certain sunny campus in the Deep South, but whose sole asset in connection with this story (apart from a slight resemblance to a long-dead great-uncle of mine) is that his appearance is out of date. Now if one is perfectly honest with oneself, there is nothing extraordinary in the tendency to

give to the manners and clothes of a distant day (which happens to be placed in the future) an old-fashioned tinge, a
badly pressed, badly groomed, dusty something, since the
terms "out of date," "not of our age," and so on are in the
long run the only ones in which we are able to imagine and
express a strangeness no amount of research can foresee. The
future is but the obsolete in reverse.

In that shabby room, in the tawny lamplight, Lance talks
of some last things. He has recently brought from a desolate
spot in the Andes, where he has been climbing some as yet
unnamed peak, a couple of adolescent chinchillas—cinder-
gray, phenomenally furry, rabbit-sized rodents *(Hystricomor-
pha)*, with long whiskers, round rumps, and petal-like ears.
He keeps them indoors in a wire-screened pen and gives
them peanuts, puffed rice, raisins to eat, and, as a special treat,
a violet or an aster. He hopes they will breed in the fall. He
now repeats to his mother a few emphatic instructions—to
keep his pets' food crisp and their pen dry, and never forget
their daily dust bath (fine sand mixed with powdered chalk)
in which they roll and kick most lustily. While this is being
discussed, Mr. Boke lights and relights a pipe and finally puts
it away. Every now and then, with a false air of benevolent
absentmindedness, the old man launches upon a series of
sounds and motions that deceive nobody; he clears his throat
and, with his hands behind his back, drifts toward a window;
or he begins to produce a tight-lipped tuneless humming;
and seemingly driven by that small nasal motor, he wanders
out of the parlor. But no sooner has he left the stage than
he throws off, with a dreadful shiver, the elaborate structure
of his gentle, bumbling impersonation act. In a bedroom or
bathroom, he stops as if to take, in abject solitude, a deep
spasmodic draft from some secret flask, and presently staggers
out again, drunk with grief.

The stage has not changed when he quietly returns to it, buttoning his coat and resuming that little hum. It is now a matter of minutes. Lance inspects the pen before he goes, and leaves Chin and Chilla sitting on their haunches, each holding a flower. The only other thing that I know about these last moments is that any such talk as "Sure you haven't forgotten the silk shirt that came from the wash?" or "You remember where you put those new slippers?" is excluded. Whatever Lance takes with him is already collected at the mysterious and unmentionable and absolutely awful place of his zero-hour departure; he needs nothing of what we need; and he steps out of the house, empty-handed and hatless, with the casual lightness of one walking to the newsstand—or to a glorious scaffold.

3

Terrestrial space loves concealment. The most it yields to the eye is a panoramic view. The horizon closes upon the receding traveler like a trap door in slow motion. For those who remain, any town a day's journey from here is invisible, whereas you can easily see such transcendencies as, say, a lunar amphitheater and the shadow cast by its circular ridge. The conjuror who displays the firmament has rolled up his sleeves and performs in full view of the little spectators. Planets may dip out of sight (just as objects are obliterated by the blurry curve of one's own cheekbone); but they are back when the earth turns its head. The nakedness of the night is appalling. Lance has left; the fragility of his young limbs grows in direct ratio to the distance he covers. From their balcony, the old Bokes look at the infinitely perilous night sky and wildly envy the lot of fishermen's wives.

If Boke's sources are accurate, the name "Lanceloz del Lac" occurs for the first time in Verse 3676 of the twelfth-century *Roman de la Charrette*. Lance, Lancelin, Lancelotik—diminutives murmured at the brimming, salty, moist stars. Young knights in their teens learning to harp, hawk, and hunt; the Forest Dangerous and the Dolorous Tower; Aldebaran, Betelgeuse—the thunder of Saracenic war cries. Marvelous deeds of arms, marvelous warriors, sparkling within the awful constellations above the Bokes' balcony: Sir Percard the Black Knight, and Sir Perimones the Red Knight, and Sir Pertolepe the Green Knight, and Sir Persant the Indigo Knight, and that bluff old party Sir Grummore Grummursum, muttering northern oaths under his breath. The field glass is not much good, the chart is all crumpled and damp, and: "You do not hold the flashlight properly"—this to Mrs. Boke.

Draw a deep breath. Look again.

Lancelot is gone; the hope of seeing him in life is about equal to the hope of seeing him in eternity. Lancelot is banished from the country of L'Eau Grise (as we might call the Great Lakes) and now rides up in the dust of the night sky almost as far as our local universe (with the balcony and the pitch-black, optically spotted garden) speeds toward King Arthur's Harp, where Vega burns and beckons—one of the few objects that can be identified by the aid of this goddam diagram. The sidereal haze makes the Bokes dizzy—gray incense, insanity, infinity-sickness. But they cannot tear themselves away from the nightmare of space, cannot go back to the lighted bedroom, a corner of which shows in the glass door. And presently *the* planet rises, like a tiny bonfire.

There, to the right, is the Bridge of the Sword leading to the Otherworld *("dont nus estranges ne retorne")*. Lancelot crawls over it in great pain, in ineffable anguish. "Thou shalt not pass a pass that is called the Pass Perilous." But another enchanter commands: "You shall. You shall even acquire a sense of humor that will tide you over the trying spots." The brave old Bokes think they can distinguish Lance scaling, on crampons, the verglased rock of the sky or silently breaking trail through the soft snows of nebulae. Boötes, somewhere between Camp X and XI, is a great glacier all rubble and ice-fall. We try to make out the serpentine route of ascent; seem to distinguish the light leanness of Lance among the several roped silhouettes. Gone! Was it he or Denny (a young biologist, Lance's best friend)? Waiting in the dark valley at the foot of the vertical sky, we recall (Mrs. Boke more clearly than her husband) those special names for crevasses and Gothic structures of ice that Lance used to mouth with such professional gusto in his alpine boyhood (he is several light-years older by now); the *séracs* and the *schrunds;* the avalanche and its thud; French echoes and Germanic magic hobnailnobbing up there as they do in medieval romances.

Ah, there he is again! Crossing through a notch between two stars; then, very slowly, attempting a traverse on a cliff face so sheer, and with such delicate holds that the mere evocation of those groping fingertips and scraping boots fills one with acrophobic nausea. And through streaming tears the old Bokes see Lance now marooned on a shelf of stone and now climbing again and now, dreadfully safe, with his ice axe and pack, on a peak above peaks, his eager profile rimmed with light.

Or is he already on his way down? I assume that no news comes from the explorers and that the Bokes prolong their pathetic vigils. As they wait for their son to return, his every avenue of descent seems to run into the precipice of their despair. But perhaps he has swung over those high-angled wet slabs that fall away vertically into the abyss, has mastered the overhang, and is now blissfully glissading down steep celestial snows?

As, however, the Bokes' doorbell does not ring at the logical culmination of an imagined series of footfalls (no matter how patiently we space them as they come nearer and nearer in our mind), we have to thrust him back and have him start his ascent all over again, and then put him even farther back, so that he is still at headquarters (where the tents are, and the open latrines, and the begging, black-footed children) long after we had pictured him bending under the tulip tree to walk up the lawn to the door and the doorbell. As if tired by the many appearances he has made in his parents' minds, Lance now plows wearily through mud puddles, then up a hillside, in the haggard landscape of a distant war, slipping and scrambling up the dead grass of the slope. There is some routine rock work ahead, and then the summit. The ridge is won. Our losses are heavy. How is one notified? By wire? By registered letter? And who is the executioner—a special messenger or the regular plodding, florid-nosed postman, always a little high (he has troubles of his own)? Sign here. Big thumb. Small cross. Weak pencil. Its dull-violet wood. Return it. The illegible signature of teetering disaster.

But nothing comes. A month passes. Chin and Chilla are in fine shape and seem very fond of each other—sleep together in the nest box, cuddled up in a fluffy ball. After many tries, Lance had discovered a sound with definite chinchillan appeal, produced by pursing the lips and emitting in rapid succession several soft, moist *surpths,* as if taking sips from a straw when most of one's drink is finished and only its dregs are drained. But his parents cannot produce it—the pitch is wrong or something. And there is such an intolerable silence in Lance's room, with its battered books, and the spotty white shelves, and the old shoes, and the relatively new tennis racquet in its preposterously secure press, and a penny on the closet floor— and all this begins to undergo a prismatic dissolution, but then you tighten the screw and everything is again in focus. And presently the Bokes return to their balcony. Has he reached his goal—and if so, does he see us?

4

The classical ex-mortal leans on his elbow from a flowered ledge to contemplate this earth, this toy, this teetotum gyrating on slow display in its model firmament, every feature so gay and clear—the painted oceans, and the praying woman of the Baltic, and a still of the elegant Americas caught in their trapeze act, and Australia like a baby Africa lying on its side. There may be people among my coevals who half expect their spirits to look down from heaven with a shudder and a sigh at their native planet and see it girdled with latitudes, stayed with meridians, and marked, perhaps, with the fat, black, diabolically curving arrows of global wars; or, more pleasantly, spread out before their gaze like one of those picture maps of vacational Eldorados, with a reservation Indian beating a drum here, a girl clad in shorts there, conical conifers climbing the cones of mountains, and anglers all over the place.

Actually, I suppose, my young descendant on his first night out, in the imagined silence of an inimaginable world, would have to view the surface features of our globe through the depth of its atmosphere; this would mean dust, scattered reflections, haze, and all kinds of optical pitfalls, so that continents, if they appeared at all through the varying clouds, would slip by in queer disguises, with inexplicable gleams of color and unrecognizable outlines.

But all this is a minor point. The main problem is: Will the mind of the explorer survive the shock? One tries to perceive the nature of that shock as plainly as mental safety permits.

And if the mere act of imagining the matter is fraught with hideous risks, how, then, will the real pang be endured and overcome?

First of all, Lance will have to deal with the atavistic moment. Myths have become so firmly entrenched in the radiant sky that common sense is apt to shirk the task of getting at the uncommon sense behind them. Immortality must have a star to stand on if it wishes to branch and blossom and support thousands of blue-plumed angel birds all singing as sweetly as little eunuchs. Deep in the human mind, the concept of dying is synonymous with that of leaving the earth. To escape its gravity means to transcend the grave, and a man upon finding himself on another planet has really no way of proving to himself that he is not dead—that the naïve old myth has not come true.

I am not concerned with the moron, the ordinary hairless ape, who takes everything in his stride; his only childhood memory is of a mule that bit him; his only consciousness of the future a vision of board and bed. What I am thinking of is the man of imagination and science, whose courage is infinite because his curiosity surpasses his courage. Nothing will keep him back. He is the ancient *curieux,* but of a hardier build, with a ruddier heart. When it comes to exploring a celestial body, his is the satisfaction of a passionate desire to feel with his own fingers, to stroke, and inspect, and smile at, and inhale, and stroke again—with that same smile of nameless, moaning, melting pleasure—the never-before-touched matter of which the celestial object is made. Any true scientist (not, of course, the fraudulent mediocrity, whose only treasure is the ignorance he hides like a bone) should be capable of experiencing that sensuous pleasure of direct and divine knowledge. He may be twenty and he may be eighty-five but without that tingle there is no science. And of that stuff Lance is made.

Straining my fancy to the utmost, I see him surmounting the panic that the ape might not experience at all. No doubt Lance may have landed in an orange-colored dust cloud somewhere in the middle of the Tharsis desert (if it is a desert) or near some purple pool—Phoenicis or Oti (if these are lakes after all). But on the other hand . . . You see, as things go in such matters, something is sure to be solved at once, terribly and irrevocably, while other things come up one by one and are puzzled out gradually. When I was a boy . . .

When I was a boy of seven or eight, I used to dream a vaguely recurrent dream set in a certain environment, which I have never been able to recognize and identify in any rational manner, though I have seen many strange lands. I am inclined to make it serve now, in order to patch up a gaping hole, a raw wound in my story. There was nothing spectacular about that environment, nothing monstrous or even odd: just a bit of noncommittal stability represented by a bit of level ground and filmed over with a bit of neutral nebulosity; in other words, the indifferent back of a view rather than its face. The nuisance of that dream was that for some reason I could not walk *around* the view to meet it on equal terms. There lurked in the mist a mass of something—mineral matter or the like—oppressively and quite meaninglessly shaped, and, in the course of my dream, I kept filling some kind of receptacle (translated as "pail") with smaller shapes (translated as "pebbles"), and my nose was bleeding but I was too impatient and excited to do anything about it. And every time I had that dream, suddenly somebody would start screaming behind me, and I awoke screaming too, thus prolonging the initial anonymous shriek, with its initial note of rising exultation, but with no meaning attached to it any more—if there *had* been a meaning. Speaking of Lance, I would like to submit that something on the lines of my dream— But the funny thing is that as I reread what I have set down, its background, the factual memory vanishes—has vanished altogether by now—and I have no means of proving to myself that there is any personal experience behind its description. What I wanted to say was that perhaps Lance and his companions, when they reached their planet, felt something akin to my dream—which is no longer mine.

5

And they were back! A horseman, clappity-clap, gallops up the cobbled street to the Bokes' house through the driving rain and shouts out the tremendous news as he stops short at the gate, near the dripping liriodendron, while the Bokes come tearing out of the house like two hystricomorphic rodents. They are back! The pilots, and the astrophysicists, and one of the naturalists, are back (the other, Denny, is dead and has been left in heaven, the old myth scoring a curious point there).

On the sixth floor of a provincial hospital, carefully hidden from newspapermen, Mr. and Mrs. Boke are told that their boy is in a little waiting room, second to the right, ready to receive them; there is something, a kind of hushed deference, about the tone of this information, as if it referred to a fairy-tale king. They will enter quietly; a nurse, a Mrs. Coover, will be there all the time. Oh, he's all right, they are told—can go home next week, as a matter of fact. However, they should not stay more than a couple of minutes, and no questions, please—just chat about something or other. *You* know. And then say you will be coming again tomorrow or day after tomorrow.

Lance, gray-robed, crop-haired, tan gone, changed, unchanged, changed, thin, nostrils stopped with absorbent cotton, sits on the edge of a couch, his hands clasped, a little embarrassed. Gets up wavily, with a beaming grimace, and sits down again. Mrs. Coover, the nurse, has blue eyes and no chin.

A ripe silence. Then Lance: "It was wonderful. Perfectly wonderful. I am going back in November."

Pause.

"I think," says Mr. Boke, "that Chilla is with child."

Quick smile, little bow of pleased acknowledgment. Then, in a narrative voice: *"Je vais dire ça en français. Nous venions d'arriver—"*

"Show them the President's letter," says Mrs. Coover.

"We had just got there," Lance continues, "and Denny was still alive, and the first thing he and I saw—"

In a sudden flutter, Nurse Coover interrupts: "No, Lance, no. No, Madam, please. No contacts, doctor's orders, *please.*"

Warm temple, cold ear.

Mr. and Mrs. Boke are ushered out. They walk swiftly—although there is no hurry, no hurry whatever, down the corridor, along its shoddy, olive-and-ochre wall, the lower olive separated from the upper ochre by a continuous brown line leading to the venerable elevators. Going up (glimpse of patriarch in wheelchair). Going back in November (Lancelin). Going down (the old Bokes). There are, in that elevator, two smiling women and, the object of their bright sympathy, a girl with a baby, besides the gray-haired, bent, sullen elevator man, who stands with his back to everybody.

Chapter Twelve

from SPEAK, MEMORY

1

When I first met Tamara—to give her a name concolorous with her real one—she was fifteen, and I was a year older. The place was the rugged but comely country (black fir, white birch, peatbogs, hayfields, and barrens) just south of St. Petersburg. A distant war was dragging on. Two years later, that trite *deus ex machina,* the Russian Revolution, came, causing my removal from the unforgettable scenery. In fact, already then, in July 1915, dim omens and backstage rumblings, the hot breath of fabulous upheavals, were affecting the so-called "Symbolist" school of Russian poetry—especially the verse of Alexander Blok.

During the beginning of that summer and all through the previous one, Tamara's name had kept cropping up (with the feigned naïveté so typical of Fate, when meaning business) here and there on our estate (Entry Forbidden) and on my uncle's land (Entry Strictly Forbidden) on the opposite bank of the Oredezh. I would find it written with a stick on the reddish sand of a park avenue, or penciled on a whitewashed wicket, or freshly carved (but not completed) in the wood of some ancient bench, as if Mother Nature were giving me mysterious advance notices of Tamara's existence. That hushed July afternoon, when I discovered her standing quite still (only her eyes were moving) in a birch grove, she seemed to have been spontaneously generated there, among those watchful trees, with the silent completeness of a mythological manifestation.

She slapped dead the horsefly that she had been waiting for to light and proceeded to catch up with two other, less pretty girls who were calling to her. Presently, from a vantage point above the river, I saw them walking over the bridge, clicking along on brisk high heels, all three with their hands tucked into the pockets of their navy-blue jackets and, because of the flies, every now and then tossing their beribboned and beflowered heads. Very soon I traced Tamara to the modest *dachka* (summer cottage) that her family rented in the village. I would ride my horse or my bicycle in the vicinity, and with the sudden sensation of a dazzling explosion (after which my heart would take quite a time to get back from where it had landed) I used to come across Tamara at this or that bland bend of the road. Mother Nature eliminated first one of her girl companions, then the other, but not until August— August 9, 1915, to be Petrarchally exact, at half-past four of that season's fairest afternoon in the rainbow-windowed pavilion that I had noticed my trespasser enter—not until then, did I muster sufficient courage to speak to her.

Seen through the carefully wiped lenses of time, the beauty of her face is as near and as glowing as ever. She was short and a trifle on the plump side but very graceful, with her slim ankles and supple waist. A drop of Tatar or Circassian blood might have accounted for the slight slant of her merry dark eye and the duskiness of her blooming cheek. A light down, akin to that found on fruit of the almond group, lined her profile with a fine rim of radiance. She accused her

rich-brown hair of being unruly and oppressive and threatened to have it bobbed, and did have it bobbed a year later,
but I always recall it as it looked first, fiercely braided into a
thick plait that was looped up at the back of her head and tied
there with a big bow of black silk. Her lovely neck was always
bare, even in winter in St. Petersburg, for she had managed to
obtain permission to eschew the stifling collar of a Russian
schoolgirl's uniform. Whenever she made a funny remark or
produced a jingle from her vast store of minor poetry, she had
a most winning way of dilating her nostrils with a little snort
of amusement. Still, I was never quite sure when she was
serious and when she was not. The rippling of her ready
laughter, her rapid speech, the roll of her very uvular *r*, the
tender, moist gleam on her lower eyelid—indeed, all her features were ecstatically fascinating to me, but somehow or
other, instead of divulging her person, they tended to form a
brilliant veil in which I got entangled every time I tried to
learn more about her. When I used to tell her we would
marry in the last days of 1917, as soon as I had finished
school, she would quietly call me a fool. I visualized her
home but vaguely. Her mother's first name and patronymic
(which were all I knew of the woman) had merchant-class
or clerical connotations. Her father, who, I gathered, took
hardly any interest in his family, was the steward of a large
estate somewhere in the south.

Autumn came early that year. Layers of fallen leaves piled
up ankle-deep by the end of August. Velvet-black Camberwell Beauties with creamy borders sailed through the glades.
The tutor to whose erratic care my brother and I were
entrusted that season used to hide in the bushes in order to
spy upon Tamara and me with the aid of an old telescope he
had found in the attic; but in his turn, one day, the peeper was
observed by my uncle's purple-nosed old gardener Apostolski

(incidentally, a great tumbler of weeding-girls) who very kindly reported it to my mother. She could not tolerate snooping, and besides (though I never spoke to her about Tamara) she knew all she cared to know of my romance from my poems which I recited to her in a spirit of praiseworthy objectivity, and which she lovingly copied out in a special album. My father was away with his regiment; he did feel it his duty, after acquainting himself with the stuff, to ask me some rather awkward questions when he returned from the front a month later; but my mother's purity of heart had carried her, and was to carry her, over worse difficulties. She contented her-self with shaking her head dubiously though not untenderly, and telling the butler to leave every night some fruit for me on the lighted veranda.

I took my adorable girl to all those secret spots in the woods, where I had daydreamed so ardently of meeting her, of creating her. In one particular pine grove everything fell into place, I parted the fabric of fancy, I tasted reality. As my uncle was absent that year, we could also stray freely in his huge, dense, two-century-old park with its classical cripples of green-stained stone in the main avenue and labyrinthine paths radiating from a central fountain. We walked "swing-ing hands," country-fashion. I picked dahlias for her on the borders along the gravel drive, under the distant benevolent eye of old Priapostolski. We felt less safe when I used to see her home, or near-home, or at least to the village bridge. I remember the coarse graffiti linking our first names, in strange diminutives, on a certain white gate and, a little apart from that village-idiot scrawl, the adage "Prudence is the friend of Passion," in a bristly hand well-known to me. Once, at sunset, near the orange and black river, a young *dachnik* (vacationist) with a riding crop in his hand bowed to her in passing; whereupon she blushed like a girl in a novel but only said, with a spirited sneer, that he had never ridden a horse in his life. And another time, as we emerged onto a turn of the highway, my two little sisters in their wild curiosity almost fell out of the red family "torpedo" swerving toward the bridge.

On dark rainy evenings I would load the lamp of my bicycle with magical lumps of calcium carbide, shield a match from the gusty wind and, having imprisoned a white flame in the glass, ride cautiously into the darkness. The circle of light cast by my lamp would pick out the damp, smooth shoulder of the road, between its central system of puddles and the long bordering grasses. Like a tottering ghost, the pale ray would weave across a clay bank at the turn as I began the downhill ride toward the river. Beyond the bridge the road sloped up again to meet the Rozhestveno-Luga highway, and just above that junction a footpath among dripping jasmin bushes ascended a steep escarpment. I had to dismount and push my bicycle. As I reached the top, my livid light flitted across the six-pillared white portico at the back of my uncle's mute, shuttered manor—as mute and shuttered as it may be today, half a century later. There, in a corner of that arched shelter, from where she had been following the zigzags of my ascending light, Tamara would be waiting, perched on the broad parapet with her back to a pillar. I would put out my lamp and grope my way toward her. One is moved to speak more eloquently about these things, about many other things that one always hopes might survive captivity in the zoo of words—but the ancient limes crowding close to the house drown Mnemosyne's monologue with their creaking and heaving in the restless night. Their sigh would subside. The rain pipe at one side of the porch, a small busybody of water, could be heard steadily bubbling. At times, some additional rustle, troubling the rhythm of the rain in the leaves, would cause Tamara to turn her head in the direction of an imagined footfall, and then, by a faint luminosity—now rising above the horizon of my memory despite all that rain—I could distinguish the outline of her face; but there was nothing and nobody to fear, and presently she would gently exhale the breath she had held for a moment and her eyes would close again.

2

With the coming of winter our reckless romance was transplanted to grim St. Petersburg. We found ourselves horribly deprived of the sylvan security we had grown accustomed to. Hotels disreputable enough to admit us stood beyond the limits of our daring, and the great era of parked amours was still remote. The secrecy that had been so pleasurable in the country now became a burden, yet neither of us could face the notion of chaperoned meetings at her home or mine. Consequently, we were forced to wander a good deal about the town (she, in her little gray-furred coat, I, white-spatted and karakul-collared, with a knuckle-duster in my velvet-lined pocket), and this permanent quest for some kind of refuge produced an odd sense of hopelessness, which, in its turn, foreshadowed other, much later and lonelier, roamings.

We skipped school: I forget what Tamara's procedure was; mine consisted of talking either of the two chauffeurs into dropping me at this or that corner on the way to school (both were good sports and actually refused to accept my gold—handy five-rouble pieces coming from the bank in appetizing, weighty sausages of ten or twenty shining pieces, in the aesthetic recollection of which I can freely indulge now that my proud émigré destitution is also a thing of the past). Nor had I any trouble with our wonderful, eminently bribable Ustin,

who took the calls on our ground-floor telephone, the number of which was 24–43, *dvadtsat' chetïre sorok tri;* he briskly
replied I had a sore throat. I wonder, by the way, what would
happen if I put in a long-distance call from my desk right
now? No answer? No such number? No such country? Or
the voice of Ustin saying *"moyo pochtenietse!"* (the ingratiating
diminutive of "my respects")? There exist, after all, well-
publicized Slavs and Kurds who are well over one hundred
and fifty. My father's telephone in his study (584–51) was not
listed, and my form master in his attempts to learn the truth
about my failing health never got anywhere, though sometimes I missed three days in a row.

We walked under the white lacery of berimed avenues in
public parks. We huddled together on cold benches—after
having removed first their tidy cover of snow, then our snow-
incrusted mittens. We haunted museums. They were drowsy
and deserted on weekday mornings, and very warm, in contrast to the glacial haze and its red sun that, like a flushed
moon, hung in the eastern windows. There we would seek
the quiet back rooms, the stopgap mythologies nobody looked
at, the etchings, the medals, the paleographic items, the Story
of Printing—poor things like that. Our best find, I think, was
a small room where brooms and ladders were kept; but a
batch of empty frames that suddenly started to slide and top-
ple in the dark attracted an inquisitive art lover, and we fled.
The Hermitage, St. Petersburg's Louvre, offered nice nooks,
especially in a certain hall on the ground floor, among cabinets with scarabs, behind the sarcophagus of Nana, high priest
of Ptah. In the Russian Museum of Emperor Alexander III,
two halls (Nos. 30 and 31, in its northeastern corner), har-
boring repellently academic paintings by Shishkin ("Clearing
in a Pine Forest") and by Harlamov ("Head of a Young
Gypsy"), offered a bit of privacy because of some tall stands

with drawings—until a foul-mouthed veteran of the Turkish campaign threatened to call the police. So from these great museums we graduated to smaller ones, such as the Suvorov, for instance, where I recall a most silent room full of old armor and tapestries, and torn silk banners, with several bewigged, heavily booted dummies in green uniforms standing guard over us. But wherever we went, invariably, after a few visits, this or that hoary, blear-eyed, felt-soled attendant would grow suspicious and we would have to transfer our furtive frenzy elsewhere—to the Pedagogical Museum, to the Museum of Court Carriages, or to a tiny museum of old maps, which guidebooks do not even list—and then out again into the cold, into some lane of great gates and green lions with rings in their jaws, into the stylized snowscape of the "Art World," *Mir Iskusstva*—Dobuzhinski, Alexandre Benois—so dear to me in those days.

On late afternoons, we got into the last row of seats in one of the two movie theaters (the Parisiana and the Piccadilly) on Nevski Avenue. The art was progressing. Sea waves were tinted a sickly blue and as they rode in and burst into foam against a black, remembered rock (Rocher de la Vierge, Biarritz—funny, I thought, to see again the beach of my cosmopolitan childhood), there was a special machine that imitated the sound of the surf, making a kind of washy swish that never quite managed to stop short with the scene but for three or four seconds accompanied the next feature—a brisk funeral, say, or shabby prisoners of war with their dapper captors. As often as not, the title of the main picture was a quotation from some popular poem or song and might be quite long-winded, such as *The Chrysanthemums Blossom No More in the Garden* or *Her Heart Was a Toy in His Hands and Like a Toy It Got Broken*. Female stars had low foreheads, magnificent eyebrows, lavishly shaded eyes. The favorite actor of the day was Mozzhuhin. One famous director had acquired in the Moscow countryside a white-pillared mansion (not unlike that of my uncle), and it appeared in all the pictures he made. Mozzhuhin would drive up to it in a smart sleigh and fix a steely eye on a light in one window while a celebrated little muscle twitched under the tight skin of his jaw.

When museums and movie houses failed us and the night was young, we were reduced to exploring the wilderness of the world's most gaunt and enigmatic city. Solitary street lamps were metamorphosed into sea creatures with prismatic spines by the icy moisture on our eyelashes. As we crossed the vast squares, various architectural phantoms arose with silent suddenness right before us. We felt a cold thrill, generally associated not with height but with depth—with an abyss opening at one's feet—when great, monolithic pillars of polished granite (polished by slaves, repolished by the moon, and rotating smoothly in the polished vacuum of the night) zoomed above us to support the mysterious rotundities of St. Isaac's cathedral. We stopped on the brink, as it were, of these perilous massifs of stone and metal, and with linked hands, in Lilliputian awe, craned our heads to watch new colossal visions rise in our way—the ten glossy-gray atlantes of a palace portico, or a giant vase of porphyry near the iron gate of a garden, or that enormous column with a black angel on its summit that obsessed, rather than adorned, the moon-flooded Palace Square, and went up and up, trying in vain to reach the subbase of Pushkin's *"Exegi monumentum."*

She contended afterward, in her rare moments of moodiness, that our love had not withstood the strain of that winter; a flaw had appeared, she said. Through all those months, I had kept writing verse to her, for her, about her, two or three poems per week; in the spring of 1916 I published a collection of them—and was horrified when she drew my attention to something I had not noticed at all when concocting the book. There it was, the same ominous flaw, the banal hollow note, and glib suggestion that our love was doomed since it could never recapture the miracle of its initial moments, the rustle and rush of those limes in the rain, the compassion of the wild countryside. Moreover—but this neither of us saw at the time—my poems were juvenile stuff, quite devoid of merit and ought never to have been put on sale. The book (a copy of which still exists, alas, in the "closed stacks" of the Lenin Library, Moscow) deserved what it got at the tearing claws of the few critics who noticed it in obscure periodicals. My Russian literature teacher at school, Vladimir Hippius, a first-rate though somewhat esoteric poet whom I greatly admired (he surpassed in talent, I think, his much better known cousin, Zinaïda Hippius, woman poet and critic) brought a copy with him to class and provoked the delirious hilarity of the majority of my classmates by applying his fiery sarcasm (he was a fierce man with red hair) to my most romantic lines. His famous cousin at a session of the Literary Fund asked my father, its president, to tell me, please, that I would never, never be a writer. A well-meaning, needy and talentless journalist, who had reasons to be grateful to my father, wrote an impossibly enthusiastic piece about me, some five hundred lines dripping with fulsome praise; it was intercepted in time by my father, and I remember him and me, while we read it in manuscript, grinding our teeth and groaning—the ritual adopted by our family when faced by something in awful taste or by somebody's *gaffe*. The whole business cured me permanently of all interest in literary fame and was probably the cause of that almost pathological and not always justified indifference to reviews which in later years deprived me of the emotions most authors are said to experience.

That spring of 1916 is the one I see as the very type of a

St. Petersburg spring, when I recall such specific images as
Tamara, wearing an unfamiliar white hat, among the spectators of a hard-fought interscholastic soccer game, in which,
that Sunday, the most sparkling luck helped me to make save
after save in goal; and a Camberwell Beauty, exactly as old as
our romance, sunning its bruised black wings, their borders
now bleached by hibernation, on the back of a bench in
Alexandrovski Garden; and the booming of cathedral bells in
the keen air, above the corrugated dark blue of the Neva,
voluptuously free of ice; and the fair in the confetti-studded
slush of the Horse Guard Boulevard during Catkin Week,
with its squeaking and popping din, its wooden toys, its loud
hawking of Turkish delight and Cartesian devils called
amerikanskie zhiteli ("American inhabitants")—minute gob-
lins of glass riding up and down in glass tubes filled with
pink- or lilac-tinted alcohol as real Americans do (though all
the epithet meant was "outlandish") in the shafts of transparent skyscrapers as the office lights go out in the greenish sky.
The excitement in the streets made one drunk with desire for
the woods and the fields. Tamara and I were especially eager
to return to our old haunts, but all through April her mother
kept wavering between renting the same cottage again and
economically staying in town. Finally, under a certain condition (accepted by Tamara with the fortitude of Hans Ander-
sen's little mermaid), the cottage was rented, and a glorious
summer immediately enveloped us, and there she was, my
happy Tamara, on the points of her toes, trying to pull down
a racemosa branch in order to pick its puckered fruit, with all
the world and its trees wheeling in the orb of her laughing
eye, and a dark patch from her exertions in the sun forming
under her raised arm on the raw shantung of her yellow
frock. We lost ourselves in mossy woods and bathed in a
fairy-tale cove and swore eternal love by the crowns of flow-

ers that, like all little Russian mermaids, she was so fond of weaving, and early in the fall she moved to town in search of a job (this was the condition set by her mother), and in the course of the following months I did not see her at all, engrossed as I was in the kind of varied experience which I thought an elegant *littérateur* should seek. I had already entered an extravagant phase of sentiment and sensuality, that was to last about ten years. In looking at it from my present tower I see myself as a hundred different young men at once, all pursuing one changeful girl in a series of simultaneous or overlapping love affairs, some delightful, some sordid, that ranged from one-night adventures to protracted involvements and dissimulations, with very meager artistic results. Not only is the experience in question, and the shadows of all those charming ladies useless to me now in recomposing my past, but it creates a bothersome defocalization, and no matter how I worry the screws of memory, I cannot recall the way Tamara and I parted. There is possibly another reason, too, for this blurring: we had parted too many times before. During that last summer in the country, we used to part forever after each secret meeting when, in the fluid blackness of the night, on that old wooden bridge between masked moon and misty river, I would kiss her warm, wet eyelids and rain-chilled face, and immediately after go back to her for yet another farewell—and then the long, dark, wobbly uphill ride, my slow, laboriously pedaling feet trying to press down the monstrously strong and resilient darkness that refused to stay under.

I do remember, however, with heartbreaking vividness, a certain evening in the summer of 1917 when, after a winter of incomprehensible separation, I chanced to meet Tamara on a suburban train. For a few minutes between two stops, in the vestibule of a rocking and rasping car, we stood next to each other, I in a state of intense embarrassment, of crushing regret, she consuming a bar of chocolate, methodically break- ing off small, hard bits of the stuff, and talking of the office where she worked. On one side of the tracks, above bluish bogs, the dark smoke of burning peat was mingling with the smoldering wreck of a huge, amber sunset. It can be proved, I think, by published records that Alexander Blok was even then noting in his diary the very peat smoke I saw, and the wrecked sky. There was later a period in my life when I might have found this relevant to my last glimpse of Tamara as she turned on the steps to look back at me before descending into the jasmin-scented, cricket-mad dusk of a small station; but today no alien marginalia can dim the purity of the pain.

3

When, at the end of the year, Lenin took over, the Bolshe- viks immediately subordinated everything to the retention of power, and a regime of bloodshed, concentration camps, and hostages entered upon its stupendous career. At the time many believed one could fight Lenin's gang and save the achievements of the March Revolution. My father, who had been elected to the Constituent Assembly which, in its pre- liminary phase, strove to prevent the entrenchment of the Soviets, decided to remain as long as possible in St. Petersburg but to send his large family to the Crimea, a region that was still free (this freedom was to last for only a few weeks longer). We traveled in two parties, my brother and I going separately from my mother and the three younger children. The Soviet era was a dull week old; liberal newspapers still came out; and while seeing us off at the Nikolaevski station and waiting with us, my imperturbable father settled down at a corner table in the buffet to write, in his flowing, "celestial" hand (as the typesetters said, marveling at the absence of corrections), a leading article for the moribund *Rech* (or perhaps some emergency publication) on those special long strips of ruled paper, which corresponded proportionally to columns of print. As far as I remember, the main reason for sending my brother and me off so promptly was the probability of our being inducted into the new "Red" army if we stayed in town. I was annoyed at going to a fascinating region in mid-November, long after the collecting season was over, having never been very good at digging for pupae (though, eventually, I did turn up a few beneath a big oak in our Crimean garden). Annoyance changed to distress, when after making a precise little cross over the face of each of us, my father rather casually added that very possibly, *ves'ma vozmozhno,* he would never see us again; whereupon, in trench coat and khaki cap, with his briefcase under his arm, he strode away into the steamy fog.

The long journey southward started tolerably well, with the heat still humming and the lamps still intact in the Petrograd–Simferopol first-class sleeper, and a passably famous singer in dramatic makeup, with a bouquet of chrysanthemums in brown paper pressed to her breast, stood in the corridor, tapping upon the pane, along which somebody walked and waved as the train started to glide, without one jolt to indicate we were leaving that gray city forever. But soon after Moscow, all comfort came to an end. At several points of our slow dreary progression, the train, including our sleeping car, was invaded by more or less Bolshevized soldiers who were returning to their homes from the front (one called them either "deserters" or "Red Heroes," depending upon one's political views). My brother and I thought it rather fun to lock ourselves up in our compartment and thwart every attempt to disturb us. Several soldiers traveling on the roof of the car added to the sport by trying to use, not unsuccessfully, the ventilator of our room as a toilet. My brother, who was a first-rate actor, managed to simulate all the symptoms of a bad case of typhus, and this helped us out when the door finally gave way. Early on the third morning, at a vague stop, I took advantage of a lull in those merry proceedings to get a breath of fresh air. I moved gingerly along the crowded corridor, stepping over the bodies of snoring men, and got off. A milky mist hung over the platform of an anonymous station—we were somewhere not far from Kharkov. I wore spats and a derby. The cane I carried, a collector's item that had belonged to my uncle Ruka, was of a light-colored, beautifully freckled wood, and the knob was a smooth pink globe of coral cupped in a gold coronet. Had I been one of the tragic bums who lurked in the mist of that station platform where a brittle young fop was pacing back and forth, I would not have withstood the temptation to destroy him. As I was about to board the train, it gave a jerk and started to move; my foot slipped and my cane was sent flying under the wheels. I had no special affection for the thing (in fact, I carelessly lost it a few years later), but I was being watched, and the fire of adolescent *amour propre* prompted me to do what I cannot imagine my present self ever doing. I waited for one, two, three, four cars to pass (Russian trains were notoriously slow in gaining momentum) and when, at last, the rails were revealed, I picked up my cane from between them and raced after the nightmarishly receding bumpers. A sturdy proletarian arm conformed to the rules of sentimental fiction (rather than to those of Marxism) by helping me to swarm up. Had I been left behind, those rules might still have held good, since I would have been brought near Tamara, who by that time had also moved south and was living in a Ukrainian hamlet less than a hundred miles from the scene of that ridiculous occurrence.

4

Of her whereabouts I learned unexpectedly a month or so after my arrival in southern Crimea. My family settled in the vicinity of Yalta, at Gaspra, near the village of Koreiz. The whole place seemed completely foreign; the smells were not Russian, the sounds were not Russian, the donkey braying every evening just as the muezzin started to chant from the village minaret (a slim blue tower silhouetted against a peach-colored sky) was positively Baghdadian. And there was I standing on a chalky bridle path near a chalky stream bed where separate, serpentlike bands of water thinly glided over oval stones—there was I, holding a letter from Tamara. I looked at the abrupt Yayla Mountains, covered up to their rocky brows with the karakul of the dark Tauric pine; at the maquis-like stretch of evergreen vegetation between mountain and sea; at the translucent pink sky, where a self-conscious crescent shone, with a single humid star near it; and the whole artificial scene struck me as something in a prettily illustrated, albeit sadly abridged, edition of *The Arabian Nights*. Suddenly I felt all the pangs of exile. There had been the case of Pushkin, of course—Pushkin who had wandered in banishment here, among those naturalized cypresses and laurels—but though some prompting might have come from his elegies, I do not think my exaltation was a pose. Thenceforth for several years, until the writing of a novel relieved me of that fertile emotion, the loss of my country was equated for me with the loss of my love.

Meanwhile, the life of my family had completely changed.

Except for a few jewels astutely buried in the normal filling of a talcum powder container, we were absolutely ruined. But this was a very minor matter. The local Tatar government had been swept away by a brand-new Soviet, and we were subjected to the preposterous and humiliating sense of utter insecurity. During the winter of 1917–18 and well into the windy and bright Crimean spring, idiotic death toddled by our side. Every other day, on the white Yalta pier (where, as you remember, the lady of Chekhov's "Lady with the Lap-dog" lost her lorgnette among the vacational crowd), various harmless people had, in advance, weights attached to their feet and then were shot by tough Bolshevik sailors imported from Sebastopol for the purpose. My father, who was not harmless, had joined us by this time, after some dangerous adventures, and, in that region of lung specialists, had adopted the mimetic disguise of a doctor without changing his name ("simple and elegant," as a chess annotator would have said of a corresponding move on the board). We dwelt in an inconspicuous villa that a kind friend, Countess Sofia Panin, had placed at our disposal. On certain nights, when rumors of nearing assassins were especially strong, the men of our family took turns patrolling the house. The slender shadows of oleander leaves would cautiously move in the sea breeze along a pale wall, as if pointing at something, with a great show of stealth. We had a shotgun and a Belgian automatic, and did our best to pooh-pooh the decree which said that anyone unlawfully possessing firearms would be executed on the spot.

Chance treated us kindly; nothing happened beyond the shock we got in the middle of a January night, when a brigand-like figure, all swathed in leather and fur, crept into our midst—but it turned out to be only our former chauffeur, Tsiganov, who had thought nothing of riding all the way from St. Petersburg, on buffers and in freight cars, through the immense, frosty and savage expanse of Russia, for the mere purpose of bringing us a very welcome sum of money unexpectedly sent us by some good friends of ours. He also brought the mail received at our St. Petersburg address; among it was that letter from Tamara. After a month's stay, Tsiganov declared the Crimean scenery bored him and departed—to go all the way back north, with a big bag over his shoulder, containing various articles which we would have gladly given him had we thought he coveted them (such as a trouser press, tennis shoes, nightshirts, an alarm clock, a flatiron, several other ridiculous things I have forgotten) and the absence of which only gradually came to light if not pointed out, with vindictive zeal, by an anemic servant girl whose pale charms he had also rifled. Curiously enough, he had prevailed upon us to transfer my mother's precious stones from the talcum powder container (that he had at once detected) to a hole dug in the garden under a versatile oak—and there they all were after his departure.

Then, one spring day in 1918, when the pink puffs of blossoming almond trees enlivened the dark mountainside, the Bolsheviks vanished and a singularly silent army of Germans replaced them. Patriotic Russians were torn between the animal relief of escaping native executioners and the necessity of owing their reprieve to a foreign invader—especially to the Germans. The latter, however, were losing their war in the west and came to Yalta on tiptoe, with diffident smiles, an army of gray apparitions easy for a patriot to ignore, and ignored it was, save for some rather ungrateful snickers at the halfhearted KEEP OFF THE GRASS signs that appeared on park lawns. A couple of months later, having nicely repaired the plumbing in various villas vacated by commissars, the Germans faded out in their turn; the Whites trickled in from the east and soon began fighting the Red Army, which was attacking the Crimea from the north. My father became Minister of Justice in the Regional Government located in Simferopol, and his family was lodged near Yalta on the Livadia grounds, the Tsar's former domain. A brash, hectic gaiety associated with White-held towns brought back, in a vulgarized version, the amenities of peaceful years. Cafés did a wonderful business. All kinds of theaters thrived. One morning, on a mountain trail, I suddenly met a strange cavalier, clad in a Circassian costume, with a tense, perspiring face painted a fantastic yellow. He kept furiously tugging at his horse, which, without heeding him, proceeded down the steep path at a curiously purposeful walk, like that of an offended person leaving a party. I had seen runaway horses, but I had never seen a walkaway one before, and my astonishment was given a still more pleasurable edge when I recognized the unfortunate rider as Mozzhuhin, whom Tamara and I had so often admired on the screen. The film *Haji Murad* (after Tolstoy's tale of that gallant, rough-riding mountain chief) was being rehearsed on the mountain pastures of the range. "Stop that brute [*Derzhite proklyatoe zhivotnoe*]," he said through his teeth as he saw me, but at the same moment, with a mighty sound of crunching and crashing stones, two authentic Tatars came running down to the rescue, and I trudged on, with my butterfly net, toward the upper crags where the Euxine race of the Hippolyte Grayling was expecting me.

In that summer of 1918, a poor little oasis of miraged youth, my brother and I used to frequent the amiable and eccentric family who owned the coastal estate Oleiz. A bantering friendship soon developed between my coeval Lidia T. and me. Many young people were always around, brown-limbed braceleted young beauties, a well-known painter called Sorin, actors, a male ballet dancer, merry White Army officers, some of whom were to die quite soon, and what with beach parties, blanket parties, bonfires, a moon-spangled sea and a fair supply of Crimean Muscat Lunel, a lot of amorous fun went on; and all the while, against this frivolous, decadent and somehow unreal background (which I was pleased to believe conjured up the atmosphere of Pushkin's visit to the Crimea a century earlier), Lidia and I played a little oasal game of our own invention. The idea consisted of parodizing a biographic approach projected, as it were, into the future and thus transforming the very specious present into a kind of paralyzed past as perceived by a doddering memoirist who recalls, through a helpless haze, his acquaintance with a great writer when both were young. For instance, either Lidia or I (it was a matter of chance inspiration) might say, on the terrace after supper: "The writer liked to go out on the terrace after supper," or "I shall always remember the remark V. V. made one warm night: 'It is,' he remarked, 'a warm night'"; or, still sillier: "He was in the habit of lighting his cigarette, before smoking it"—all this delivered with much pensive, reminiscent fervor which seemed hilarious and harmless to us at the time; but now—now I catch myself wondering if we did not disturb unwittingly some perverse and spiteful demon.

Through all those months, every time a bag of mail managed to get from the Ukraine to Yalta, there would be a letter for me from my Cynara. Nothing is more occult than the way letters, under the auspices of unimaginable carriers, circulate through the weird mess of civil wars; but whenever, owing to that mess, there was some break in our correspondence, Tamara would act as if she ranked deliveries with ordinary natural phenomena such as the weather or tides, which human affairs could not affect, and she would accuse me of not answering her, when in fact I did nothing but write to her and think of her during those months—despite my many betrayals.

5

Happy is the novelist who manages to preserve an actual love letter that he received when he was young within a work of fiction, embedded in it like a clean bullet in flabby flesh and quite secure there, among spurious lives. I wish I had kept the whole of our correspondence that way. Tamara's letters were a sustained conjuration of the rural landscape we knew so well. They were, in a sense, a distant but wonderfully clear antiphonal response to the much less expressive lyrics I had once dedicated to her. By means of unpampered words, whose secret I fail to discover, her high-school-girlish prose could evoke with plangent strength every whiff of damp leaf, every autumn-rusted frond of fern in the St. Petersburg countryside. "Why did we feel so cheerful when it rained?" she asked in one of her last letters, reverting as it were to the pure source of rhetorics. *"Bozhe moy"* (*mon Dieu*—rather than "My God"), where has it gone, all that distant, bright, endearing (*Vsyo eto dalyokoe, svetloe, miloe*—in Russian no subject is needed here, since these are neuter adjectives that play the part of abstract nouns, on a bare stage, in a subdued light).

Tamara, Russia, the wildwood grading into old gardens, my northern birches and firs, the sight of my mother getting down on her hands and knees to kiss the earth every time we came back to the country from town for the summer, *et la montagne et le grand chêne*—these are things that fate one day bundled up pell-mell and tossed into the sea, completely severing me from my boyhood. I wonder, however, whether there is really much to be said for more anesthetic destinies, for, let us say, a smooth, safe, small-town continuity of time, with its primitive absence of perspective, when, at fifty, one is still dwelling in the clapboard house of one's childhood, so that every time one cleans the attic one comes across the same pile of old brown schoolbooks, still together among later accumulations of dead objects, and where, on summery Sunday mornings, one's wife stops on the sidewalk to endure for a minute or two that terrible, garrulous, dyed, church-bound McGee woman, who, way back in 1915, used to be pretty, naughty Margaret Ann of the mint-flavored mouth and nimble fingers.

The break in my own destiny affords me in retrospect a syncopal kick that I would not have missed for worlds. Ever since that exchange of letters with Tamara, homesickness has been with me a sensuous and particular matter. Nowadays, the mental image of matted grass on the Yayla, of a canyon in the Urals or of salt flats in the Aral Region, affects me nostalgically and patriotically as little, or as much, as, say, Utah; but give me anything on any continent resembling the St. Petersburg countryside and my heart melts. What it would be actually to see again my former surroundings, I can hardly imagine. Sometimes I fancy myself revisiting them with a false passport, under an assumed name. It could be done.

But I do not think I shall ever do it. I have been dreaming of it too idly and too long. Similarly, during the latter half of my sixteen-month stay in the Crimea, I planned for so long a time to join Denikin's army, with the intention not so much of clattering astride a chamfrained charger into the cobbled outskirts of St. Petersburg (my poor Yuri's dream) as of reaching Tamara in her Ukrainian hamlet, that the army ceased to exist by the time I had made up my mind. In March of 1919, the Reds broke through in northern Crimea, and from various ports a tumultuous evacuation of anti-Bolshevik groups began. Over a glassy sea in the bay of Sebastopol, under wild machine-gun fire from the shore (the Bolshevik troops had just taken the port), my family and I set out for Constantinople and Piraeus on a small and shoddy Greek ship *Nadezhda* (Hope) carrying a cargo of dried fruit. I remember trying to concentrate, as we were zigzagging out of the bay, on a game of chess with my father—one of the knights had lost its head, and a poker chip replaced a missing rook—and the sense of leaving Russia was totally eclipsed by the agonizing thought that Reds or no Reds, letters from Tamara would be still coming, miraculously and needlessly, to southern Crimea, and would search there for a fugitive addressee, and weakly flap about like bewildered butterflies set loose in an alien zone, at the wrong altitude, among an unfamiliar flora.

Ada, or Ardor

A love story troubled by incest, it is also at once a fairy tale, epic, philosophical treatise on the nature of time, parody of the history of the novel, and erotic catalog.
Fiction/Literature/0-679-72522-9

Bend Sinister

Filled with veiled puns and characteristically delightful wordplay, *Bend Sinister* is, first and foremost, a haunting and compelling narrative about a civilized man and his child caught up in the tyranny of a police state.
Fiction/Literature/0-679-72727-2

The Defense

In this chilling story of obsession and madness, Luzhin, a grandmaster who took up chess as a refuge from the anxiety of his everyday life, suddenly plummets toward madness during a crucial championship match.
Fiction/Literature/0-679-72722-1

Despair

Despair is the wickedly inventive and richly derisive story of Hermann, a man who undertakes the perfect crime: his own murder.
Fiction/Literature/0-679-72343-9

The Enchanter

At once hilarious and chilling, this starkly powerful precursor of *Lolita* tells the story of an outwardly respectable man and his fatal obsession with certain pubescent girls.
Fiction/Literature/0-679-72886-4

The Eye

As much a farcical detective story as a profoundly refractive tale, *The Eye* is the story of a man who commits suicide, then sets out in the afterlife in search of proof of his own existence.
Fiction/Literature/0-679-72723-X

The Gift

Both an ode to Russian literature and one of its major works, this is the story of Fyodor Godunov-Cherdyntsev, an impoverished émigré poet living in Berlin, who dreams of the book he will someday write—a book very much like *The Gift*.
Fiction/Literature/0-679-72725-6

Glory

Martin Edelweiss is in love with a girl who refuses to marry him. Convinced that his life is about to be wasted and hoping to impress his love, he decides to embark upon a "perilous, daredevil project"—but at a terrible cost.
Fiction/Literature/0-679-72724-8

Invitation to a Beheading

Cincinnatus C. is condemned to death by beheading for "gnostical turpitude," an imaginary crime that defies definition. Cincinnatus spends his last days in an absurd jail where he is visited by a bizarre collection of people.
Fiction/Literature/0-679-72531-8

King, Queen, Knave

Ruddy, self-satisfied, and thoroughly masculine, Dreyer is thoroughly repugnant to his exquisite but cold middle-class wife, Martha, who takes up with his newly arrived nephew, Franz, in what Nabokov called his "gayest novel."
Fiction/Literature/0-679-72340-4

Laughter in the Dark

An elegantly sardonic and irresistibly ironic novel of desire, deceit, and deception, *Laughter in the Dark* is also a curious romantic triangle set in the film world of Berlin in the 1930s.
Fiction/Literature/0-679-72450-8

Lolita

The classic story of the aging Humbert Humbert's obsessive, devouring, and doomed passion for the nymphet Dolores Haze.
Fiction/Literature/0-679-72316-1

Look at the Harlequins!

As intricate as a house of mirrors, *Look at the Harlequins!* is about Vadim, an author much like Nabokov himself, whose last novel may have crossed the line between fiction and reality.

Fiction/Literature/0-679-72728-0

Mary

In Berlin a vigorous young Russian émigré relives his love affair with Mary, his memories suffused with the freshness of youth, only to discover that the unappealing boarder next door is Mary's husband.

Fiction/Literature/0-679-72620-9

Pale Fire

In *Pale Fire,* a 999-line poem by the reclusive genius John Shade and an adoring foreword and commentary by his self-styled Boswell, Dr. Charles Kinbote, turn into a darkly comic novel of suspense, literary idolatry, and political intrigue.

Fiction/Literature/0-679-72342-0

Pnin

Pnin is a professor of a language he cannot master, a lover to his treacherous Liza, and the focal point of subtle academic conspiracies, yet he stages a faculty party to end all faculty parties forever.

Fiction/Literature/0-679-72341-2

The Real Life of Sebastian Knight

The Real Life of Sebastian Knight is a perversely magical literary detective story—subtle, intricate, leading to a tantalizing climax—about the mysterious life of a famous writer.

Fiction/Literature/0-679-72726-4

Speak, Memory

Speak, Memory is an elegant and rich remembrance of Nabokov's life and times that also offers insights into his major works.

Autobiography/Literature/0-679-72339-0

The Stories of Vladimir Nabokov

Here the stories of one of the century's greatest prose stylists are collected in a single, comprehensive volume that reminds us that we are in the presence of a magnificent original, a genuine master.

Fiction/Literature/0-679-72997-6

Strong Opinions

In this collection of interviews, articles, and editorials, Nabokov offers his trenchant, witty, and always engaging views on everything from the Russian Revolution to the correct pronunciation of *Lolita*.

Nonfiction/Literature/0-679-72609-8

Transparent Things

A novel of dreams, memory, and the past recaptured—as well as murder, madness, and imprisonment—*Transparent Things* revolves around four trancelike trips to Switzerland.

Fiction/Literature/0-679-72541-5

VINTAGE **READERS**

Authors available in this series

Martin Amis

James Baldwin

Sandra Cisneros

Joan Didion

Richard Ford

Langston Hughes

Barry Lopez

Alice Munro

Haruki Murakami

Vladimir Nabokov

V. S. Naipaul

Oliver Sacks

Representing a wide spectrum of some of our most significant
modern authors, the Vintage Readers offer an attractive,
accessible selection of writing that matters.